Two Dreams & Other Tales

◆

G. S. Treakle

Copyright © 2023   G. S. Treakle

All rights reserved. No part of this book may be used or reproduced in any manner whatsoever without written permission from the author, with the exception of short passages for review purposes.

Some of these stories contain references to actual people, places, and events. To the best of the author's knowledge, they have been portrayed accurately. All other elements of the stories, including several geographic locations, are fiction. Any similarity between fictional story elements and real-life persons or events are strictly coincidental.

ISBN: 979-8-9858078-1-3

FOREWORD

When I was a child, I had a very active imagination. I wasn't a great storyteller in the oral tradition, but my ambition was to write books for a living when I grew up. I wanted to use that medium to tell stories like the ones I spent much of my childhood creating in my head. Though I originally set my sights on a degree and career in journalism and a secondary career in creative writing, I spent four decades instead developing data and doing numerical systems analysis for the US Navy. During my career, I produced an extensive library of technical documentation, always taking pride in my skill—at least as I perceived it—as a technical writer. Still, I never lost my desire to write and tell stories. I dabbled—though not too seriously—as a writer of poems, essays, skits, comedy bits, humorous tunes, and short stories mostly for my own pleasure and the edification of friends and colleagues.

When I first saw retirement rolling down the tracks toward me, I considered what I might do with my life afterward. That was when I became serious about creative writing again. Over the last nine years, I've written more than a dozen short—and not so short—stories, completed an unfinished novella, and published my first novel, *Return to the Lion's Den*. This collection of stories represents some of my best work from that period. My hope is these tales will entertain and perhaps inspire you to write and tell stories of your own.

Greg Treakle
August 13, 2023

TABLE OF CONTENTS.

Tale #1. Passing Through 1

Tale #2. Two Dreams 35

Tale #3. Granddaddy & Me 71

Tale #4. Three Days at Sunset 101

Tale #5. My Father's Promise 139

Acknowledgements 151

TWO DREAMS & OTHER TALES

Tale #1. Passing Through

Texas, August 2013

You could tell how hot it was by looking at the heat rising off the highway up ahead. Temperatures often topped 100 degrees on the Texas plains during this part of summer. Many times, those baking conditions gave way in the afternoon to storms sweeping in from the west with rain, lightning, and the occasional twister. On this day, however, it was sunny and hot with no forecast of bad weather.

I was traveling east on State Highway 631, about an hour east of Dallas. My destination was a small town called Hillman, which was the seat of a county of the same name. Hillman sits in the middle of an extensive area of large farms and oil fields worked by small, independent operators. The land is flat and devoid of trees, making it possible to see for miles in all directions. Along that stretch of highway that day, what I saw the most of was wheat and the occasional oil field. In many of the fields, the derricks were not only silent, but abandoned. It was a troubling sign that the small operators had pulled out and didn't even take their equipment with them.

I passed a sign informing me I was six miles from my destination. Just barely visible was the water tower that dominated the sky at the northern end of town, right where this same highway crossed over Main Street. Signs of life began to appear. I passed a grain elevator on the right, followed by a heavy equipment depot full of large farming and earth-moving trucks, tractors, and other vehicles. A few minutes later, I saw trees and houses. As I came to the town limits, I passed a sign that said:

WELCOME TO HILLMAN
Population: 897

It seemed unlikely that the population of the town had not changed in the fourteen years since I had last been there. Perhaps the locals had more pressing matters to deal with than keeping that sign up to date. It was there at the town limits that State Highway 631 became Huntington Avenue. I passed a couple of small businesses and a side street with a residential

TWO DREAMS & OTHER TALES
Passing Through

neighborhood as I approached Main Street. I would need to get gas before heading back to Dallas, so I stopped at the convenience mart at the corner of Huntington and Main and pulled over to the pumps.

As the gas flowed, I looked around me, taking in some old familiar sights. It felt strange to be back in my hometown, a place I once thought I would never see again. The county public works garage stood on the opposite corner of the intersection. It was home to the crews and equipment that maintained county roads, the municipal water district, and the grounds of public facilities like the courthouse and the schools. Next door to the garage was one of three county fire stations. What was not visible from where I stood was the fenced-in area behind the garage where the water tower stood. It rose through the trees high enough to make it visible along the full length of Main Street. I recalled that this tower, which bore the name HILLMAN, was also visible from my bedroom window when I was a boy. My childhood home—which was no longer standing—had been close by.

I was born in Hillman in February 1981, the eldest child of George and Patty Welles. My given name is George Jr., but to avoid confusion over identities, my family called me Byron. My father, George Sr., was a machinist by trade. He worked oil rigs, grain elevators, heavy equipment depots, factories, and other places where machine and metal work needed doing. During my childhood years, he had many regular jobs and many temporary jobs, occasionally followed by layoffs and varying periods of unemployment. He made good money when he was working, but even then, we lived frugally to prepare for the lean times. Despite these limitations, my father was a good man and a good provider. The one thing about him I had a difficult time with was his personality. My father grew up in a family that did not share verbal and physical affection. He was a cold fish who never smiled, and I got no genuine affection from him. I never doubted he loved me, but it always hurt that he wouldn't say it.

My mother, Patty, was a tragic figure. Raised in a very religious family, she was a faithful believer. A devoted member and regular volunteer at First Baptist Church of Hillman, she practically worshipped our pastor, Reverend Doctor J. D. McCollough. She was also a good wife and mother. The tragedy of her life was that she was sick much of the time. I never

TWO DREAMS & OTHER TALES
Passing Through

understood exactly what her problem was, but she was always suffering from something. I was five years old when the word "hypochondriac" was first whispered in my presence. At first, I wasn't old enough to understand what that word meant. By the time I was, I was also old enough to understand why I did not believe that about my mother. First, she never asked for or accepted anyone's sympathy, and never used her condition to control other people. In addition, hypochondria wouldn't explain the three miscarriages she suffered during the decade that followed my birth. It was these losses that convinced me I would forever be an only child.

My mother surprised us all by giving birth to a daughter in May 1994. We named my baby sister Marcy. She was a very sweet child with an infectious laugh and a headful of red hair. Since her birth was difficult, Momma was determined that we would all protect her like she was a fragile flower. I did my part, often caring for her when my mother was out. By age three, she still could not pronounce the letter "r" so she called me "By-By." This amused everyone because they always thought she was telling me to go away. I made a joke of it, giving her the pet's name "May-May." We were always very close, despite the thirteen-year difference in our ages.

My childhood was that of an ordinary Texas youngster. Hillman was a fairly quiet place, but like kids everywhere, my friends and I always found ways to get into mischief. As a child, I was mostly a dabbler. I tried my hand at music, but couldn't hold a tune, and didn't have the discipline to master a musical instrument. I built various collections—baseball cards, stamps, coins—but eventually lost interest in each. My mother insisted that her children take part in church activities, so I faithfully attended First Baptist and took part in the youth group throughout my childhood. I took an interest in girls, but never stayed interested in any one for long. In high school, I tried athletics. But after two full seasons on the bench, I decided that football wasn't for me. It was right after football season during my sophomore year that I got a job at Fuller's Supermarket, stocking shelves, bagging groceries, and other general labor. This one stuck. Bob Fuller, my boss, was a third-generation grocer, operating the store on Main Street founded by his grandfather in 1948. I stayed with that job through the rest of high school and well into the summer that followed graduation.

TWO DREAMS & OTHER TALES
Passing Through

***

I was traveling south along Main Street, taking in more familiar sights. It amazed me how little the town had changed, like a snapshot in time held in place. A few of the old businesses were obviously closed—no doubt because of the economic downturn—but the storefronts were still there since nobody else had moved in. It pleased me that the local movie theatre was still running the latest films. My friends and I spent many Friday and Saturday nights there. I stopped at the light where Main Street intersects the aptly name School Street. Looking in one direction and then the other, I saw both of my alma maters, Hillman Primary School, and Hillman High School.

Once on the move again, I kept my gaze primarily to the right, watching for my destination. Once I saw it, I pulled into a parking space on the street out front. It was a large brick building that bore a red, white, and blue sign that identified it as the United States Post Office for Hillman, Texas. Out front, a flagpole rose from the lawn with the U.S. flag flying aloft. This is it, I told myself. Shortly after I conclude my business in there, everyone will know Byron Welles is back in town.

I stepped out of the car and made my way to the front entrance. The stenciled lettering on the glass door stated this post office had regular business hours on Monday through Friday, a half-day on Saturday, and was closed on Sunday. It also commanded patrons to wear shirts and shoes inside the facility. When I stepped into the lobby, I noted it had not changed and could pass for most any post office I'd ever been in. To the right was a worktable for people who wanted to open and examine their incoming mail or prepare their outgoing mail before sending it. Directly in front of me were mail slots for local and non-local delivery, while personal mailboxes lined the wall to the right, continuing around the corner and out of sight. I opened another glass door to the left and entered a customer service area with three service windows. Behind the windows was a wall-like partition that blocked the working area in back from customer view.

Only one window had a clerk working behind it. She was serving a customer who was apparently trying to send a large parcel to some distant place. The customer was a tall woman who had straight, bleach blonde hair and was wearing a white t-shirt, khaki shorts, and black rubber flip-flops. Perched on a couch nearby was a small child who clearly belonged to her. She was about four years old and had the same straight yellow—almost white—hair. Her clothes matched the woman's exactly, except that she had cast her footwear aside on the floor. No shoes, no service, I thought with a grin. You have to love the blissful innocence of small children. The little girl saw my smile and giggled, drawing a quick glance from her mother, who then noted my presence without expression.

    As I stood in line waiting my turn, a strange feeling of recognition crept over me. Listening to the postal clerk speak, I realized that twangy voice was familiar to me. Peering over the shoulder of the other customer, I also recognized her face, though the hair was shorter than I remembered. A look at her name plate confirmed it for me. It said Holly Kendall. *Kendall*? This woman and I attended school together and were members of the same class. In high school, many regarded Holly as a gossip, though the characterization was inaccurate. She didn't actively collect or dish other people's dirt, but she ran with classmates who did. As the loudest and most demonstrative of the bunch, she got tagged as the leader. Despite that, Holly was one of the nicest people I knew and would do just about anything for a friend, of which she had many. I was told multiple times that she *liked* me, but I never pursued her or encouraged her to pursue me.

    My most vivid memory of Holly was from the day we graduated high school. I was waiting in front of the school for my family to come out. Suddenly, this Texas tornado swept across the lawn toward me. A beautiful white knee-length dress shown from beneath her unzipped graduation gown. She was also barefoot, with a pair of strappy white high heels dangling from the fingers of her right hand. Without warning, she jumped up on tippy toes, put her free hand on my shoulder, and planted a firm kiss on my cheek. She told me the last twelve years had been loads of fun and she hoped we would be friends forever. Lest anyone think we were an item, I'm certain that several others—both boys and girls—got the same greeting that day. Needless to say, we all liked Holly. As I came back to the present, the lady customer was thanking her for her help.

TWO DREAMS & OTHER TALES
Passing Through

"Sure thing, Brenda," she said. "See you next time." The woman collected up her child, briefly nodded at me, and headed out through the lobby. My old classmate disappeared behind the partition with the parcel in hand. When she came back, she returned to her place behind the service window, looking directly at me, but giving no hint of recognition.

"May I help you, sir?" she asked.

"I suspect it's a long shot," I said, "but I'm trying to locate someone who used to live in this town. I'm hoping she left a change-of-address, and that if she did, you might still have it on file."

"How long ago are we talking about?"

"Thirteen years."

She grimaced, then shook her head back and forth. "I'm sorry, but we didn't keep changes-of-address for more than a year back then." She stopped abruptly, held up a finger, and thought for a second. "Actually, we copied a lot of old files onto the computers a few years back. It's not likely, but let me look." She turned to the computer screen on her left and stroked a couple of keys. "What is the name of the party?"

"It's my mother, Patty Welles."

She stroked a few more keys, then stopped and looked at me closely, her mouth dropping open. "Oh, my goodness. Byron! Is it really you? I'm so embarrassed. I've known you my whole life, and I didn't recognize you. You know who I am, don't you?"

"Of course. You used to be Holly Richards."

"That's me," she said with a wide smile. "How are you doing?"

"About as well as can be expected." It seemed like a safe, noncommittal answer.

She said, "I saw you on the news recently and I was wondering—" She stopped and paused. "I'm sorry, we were talking about your mother, weren't we?" She began key stroking again and continued for another moment. "I'm sorry, Byron, but she's not in here." Before I could react, she said, "Listen, it was common knowledge that your mother and sister left town without a word right after they buried your father. It was all so tragic. She had a few friends who might have heard from her since then. Another long shot, perhaps, but I could ask around for you. Are you staying here in town?"

"No, I'm not."

"Nearby?"

"I'm not staying at all," I said firmly. "I'm just passing through."

She nodded. "May I make a suggestion? You should check in with Joe Deavers. He might be able to help you out."

I remembered that name very well. He was my high school shop teacher and a mentor of sorts. I wasn't so sure about "checking in" with him, though, as I had burned that bridge a long time ago. Still, curiosity compelled me to ask, "Does he still teach at the high school?"

"Not anymore. He's a cop now with the Hillman County Sheriff."

"Seriously?" The thought of Mr. Deavers wearing a firearm amused me.

"He's been with them for about five years. I remember how much he loved all you boys. He kept up with your family after... well, you know, after you went away. He can probably fill in some blanks for you."

"I'll keep that in mind. Thanks, Holly."

As I turned to leave, she called out my name. I looked back to see her scooting past the other service windows, then coming out through the little half-door at the end. She rushed over to me, then reached out with both arms and embraced me. It wasn't one of those exaggerated shows of affection she was famous for, but a brief sisterly squeeze that lasted only a couple of seconds.

Suddenly emotional, she looked me in the eye, and quietly said, "Even though you're just passing through, I can't tell you how happy I am that they finally let you come home. You belong here and I hope you eventually come back to stay. And I really hope you find your mother. If there's any way I can help, please don't hesitate to ask."

TWO DREAMS & OTHER TALES
Passing Through

I could tell she meant every word. There was none of the flighty schoolgirl I remembered. My forever friend had grown up. I smiled and said yet again, "Thanks, Holly."

She smiled, touched her fingertips to my cheek, then retreated through the half-door, back down the line of service windows, and out of sight behind the partition.

I certainly didn't expect any of that, I thought as I headed for the exit. I became a bit disoriented by the sudden change in temperature as I passed out of the cool lobby into the oppressive midsummer heat. What really staggered me, though, was the sight I beheld when I did. I'd avoided looking at it when I came in, but now that it was directly in front of me, there was no looking away.

Across Main Street stood Hillman County Courthouse. It was a very imposing structure with a large white front door, porch columns, and a bell tower that made it look a lot like a church. However, there were no crosses on the premises and no actual bell in the tower. The brick building looked ancient, as well as it should, having stood since 1875. The previous courthouse stood on that same site before it burned during the Civil War. Though the courthouse was very historic in the literal sense, it was part of the more recent history of the place that was most significant to me. It was there in that courthouse that my childhood had abruptly ended fourteen years earlier. On a hot summer day like this one, I was convicted of a heinous crime I didn't commit. For that, I was sentenced to spend the rest of my natural life in a cage.

Though I felt sick to my stomach and weak in the knees all at once, I kept my balance as I stumbled to my borrowed car. Climbing inside, I quickly started the engine and turned the air conditioning all the way up. I leaned forward and rested my head in my hands, waiting for the queasy feeling to pass. I'd figured this day would be hard, but I hadn't expected it to be this hard. My thoughts gained a certain momentum and the terrible memories seemed determined to assert themselves, so I lowered my defenses and let them come.

***

TWO DREAMS & OTHER TALES
Passing Through

It was the summer of 1999. That year, Byron Welles, Holly Richards, and ninety-six other Hillman County teenagers graduated from high school with various plans for their futures. Mine had not originally involved college, at least not right away. My family had little money, so I wanted to go into the military for at least five years. I would learn a technical specialty, save my pennies, accumulate whatever educational benefits I could, and if required, fight for my country. If I didn't eventually choose to make the military my career, I would then go to engineering school.

The one major obstacle to this plan was my mother. While she understood the need for our country to have a military, she didn't want me anywhere near it. In keeping with her religious beliefs, she abhorred violence and did not want her son trained for such things. During the previous decade, the U.S. had been to war in Kuwait, and the madman who started all of that was still at it. Added to that, terrorists had bombed two of our embassies in Africa. My mother feared that if I joined up, I would end up fighting in the Middle East and never come back—at least not alive.

To placate her, I applied and got accepted to Texas Tech, where I planned to major in mechanical engineering. To find financing for my college education, I spent the last half of my senior year of high school researching grants, scholarships, student loans, and work-study programs. I also looked for part-time job opportunities in the Lubbock area. Part of my savings plan was to continue with my job at Fuller's Supermarket for the summer. Mr. Fuller put me on full-time and gave me a side project. He'd lost his son, Darryl, in a freak accident on an oil rig in April of that year and was still in a terrible state over it. Darryl left behind a wife named Donna and an adorable four-year-old daughter named Samantha, also known as Sammy. One ability the young Mrs. Fuller never mastered was driving a car. Without her husband, her resources and her mobility were both seriously limited. Mr. Fuller wanted his son's family provided for and paid me out of his own pocket to deliver a load of groceries to their home each week. In a small town where rumors abound, it wasn't long before I started hearing jokes about the handsome young stud hanging around the house of the pretty young widow. Such jokes weren't funny to me, but protesting would only make them louder and more persistent, so I let it go. Little did I know this arrangement would lead to my downfall.

TWO DREAMS & OTHER TALES
Passing Through

My life began to unravel on a Tuesday afternoon in July, though I didn't know it right away. That day, I got off work at 4:30 and delivered a big load of goods to the Fuller ladies. As usual, Miss Donna tried to feed me, and I politely declined. I took a few moments to visit with Sammy, who reminded me so much of my little sister. I got home about 5:30 to find that my mother and Marcy were off on an errand and my father was out on a job somewhere. After a simple dinner, I sat down with an engineering text I found at the library. I was trying to gain some perspective on what to expect in my freshman college courses.

Shortly after nightfall, the town was suddenly filled with the sound of sirens. Those who didn't hear the news that night woke the next morning to learn that the Fuller house on Oak Terrace had burned to the ground the night before. Little Sammy Fuller perished in the flames and her mother was injured trying to save her. The news absolutely devastated me. It was quickly determined that the fire was no accident; someone had set it. Investigators learned I had been there that day, so they came to speak with me. They left apparently satisfied with my answers, but returned two days later, prompted by an anonymous tip and armed with a search warrant. Nobody was more surprised than me when paraphernalia used to set arson fires turned up in the trunk of my car. Forensic testing later connected some of that evidence to the crime scene.

I was completely stunned when they led me away in handcuffs. For two days, as the town buzzed with rumors, detectives from the sheriff's department interrogated me. The evidence trail dried up quickly and what they had was problematic. The items found in my trunk had no fingerprints on them. Who would go to the trouble of sanitizing damning evidence and then keep it? There was also something troubling about having it all handed to them anonymously. Was it possible that this was a frame, and that the tipster was the real culprit? My refusal to confess frustrated the detectives. While the annals of crime are full of stories about people who falsely confessed under pressure, I had no intention of doing so. Even a forced confession can be difficult to recant.

To everyone's surprise, a very ambitious young prosecutor named Alvin Marshall tried the case, anyway. Prosecutors have won with a lot less.

TWO DREAMS & OTHER TALES
Passing Through

What worked against me was my legal representation. Don't misunderstand this. I'm not in the habit of casting aspersions on whole professions, not even the law. In fact, during my passage through the legal system, I met many good lawyers. Justice miscarried this time because of imperfect representation. My family couldn't afford legal counsel, so the court appointed me a lawyer who was so new that his law school diploma probably still had wet ink on it. The state made its case, weak though it was. The defense offered virtually no defense at all, missing several opportunities to establish reasonable doubt. In the end, a seemingly reluctant jury found me guilty. The judge gave me a mandatory life sentence without parole. As ambitious as Mr. Marshall was, he knew better than to turn the jury against him by seeking the death penalty against a likable defendant.

For me, the most awkward moment of the entire ordeal came as I was being led away for transport. On the steps of the courthouse, my mother clung to me and wept loudly. Then my father placed his arms around me and told me for the first time in my life that he loved me. I was suddenly angry with him for waiting all those years to say it. I would not return his embrace or respond in kind. As I looked at him from the back seat of the police vehicle, I saw a mixture of grief and hurt on his face and became very ashamed of myself. If I had known that I would never see him again, I would have held on for dear life.

They incarcerated me in a prison nearly 300 miles from home. With help from others, Momma made the trip to see me once. Less than a year into my term, I got an even bigger shock than that of my conviction. I learned that another arsonist—or perhaps the same one—burned our house in Hillman to the ground, and that my father died of a "cardiac event" the same night. Shortly after that, my mother and sister went off the grid, leaving no word to anybody of their destination. Nobody in Hillman ever saw or heard from them again.

It would be fourteen years before I regained my freedom. Exoneration came unexpectedly and from an unlikely source. In Hillman lived Colin Garver, a man two years older than me and fifty pounds heavier. He was literally a bruiser, raised by a violent, alcoholic father. He was the

TWO DREAMS & OTHER TALES
Passing Through

town bully, who truly hated the world around him—and everyone in it. People avoided him like the plague and those who didn't get out of his way fast enough fell victim to his abuse. I once got my lip split for looking at him the wrong way. In the summer of 2013, Colin Garver learned he was dying. Despite being relatively young at age thirty-four, twenty years of heavy drinking had left him with a failing liver. Given his lifestyle—he was also a heavy smoker—there would be no priority for him in the transplant registry.

Faced with his own mortality, Colin discovered his conscience and a hysterical fear of hell. And so, he called in a spiritual adviser in the person of Reverend Edward Chandler, the pastor at First Baptist Church of Hillman. Chandler had succeeded the old pastor, Doctor McCollough. During their sessions together, Colin confessed to many things. Most notable among them was that he set the Oak Terrace fire which killed the little Fuller girl. He also framed that Welles kid for the crime, and burned out the Welles family, hoping to drive them from town. Alerted to these confessions, the authorities set in motion events that would ultimately make me a free man.

While my case was in the appeals process, the court released me on bond to a halfway house in Dallas, just a little more than an hour's drive from Hillman. They kept me on a tight leash there, but it was boundless freedom by comparison. By coincidence, Colin Garver died the day I got out of prison. It was a mere two weeks later that I drove into Hillman for the first time in fourteen years. That was the day I visited the post office and sat in a car across from the courthouse where my odyssey first began.

***

I was driving north along Main Street, headed back the way I came. Still a bit shaken by the persistent memories of my trial, I took no more notice of familiar sights. After passing once again through the intersection at Huntington Avenue, I drove another half-mile, then turned right onto Berry Hollow Road. When I was a teenager living there, it seemed like such an odd name for a road on the Texas plains. There was no mountain in sight, much less two of them side-by-side with a hollow between them. The road had been there for so long, nobody remembered where the name came from.

TWO DREAMS & OTHER TALES
Passing Through

After a short drive, I passed through an intersection and immediately saw on the right the empty lot where our house once stood.

I stopped in the middle of the road and stared at it. The gravel driveway was still there, though a foot of scrub grass had grown up along the edges of it near the road. At the entrance was a "For Sale" sign that was old and rusty enough that I assumed it had been there for several years. I turned in and pulled to the head of the driveway. There on the ground in front of me were two flat concrete slabs. The larger one to the right had been the foundation of our small house, while the one directly in front was where the garage had stood. It was as though a tornado had swept down and wiped the slates clean. Everything I ever owned had been in that house, either burned up or claimed by someone who didn't pay for any of it.

I replayed the previous half-hour in my mind and one detail stood out: Holly's suggestion that I check in with Joe Deavers, the teacher-turned-cop. Mr. Deavers was easily the most popular teacher among boys at Hillman High. In shop class, he showed us cool gadgets that demonstrated the principles of electricity and magnetism. He also taught us to use power tools and carpentry equipment, and let us design and build our own mechanical gadgets. But what made him so popular was his effective mentoring of all his male students. He grew up with a single mother and two sisters, but no brothers. He married Maureen Stanton, daughter of a local pastor, and raised three daughters with her, but no sons. Despite the lack of males in his immediate family line, he had a gift for mentoring teenage boys. Those without fathers at home often turned to him when they needed a father figure. Those of us who did have fathers still sought him out for advice. Many of his boys kept up with him after graduation, even ones that left town.

I got out of the car and strolled around the building sites. I stood in various spots on the house slab and summoned memories from each room. Stepping into the former backyard, I looked out across the open plain, remembering the many times I watched powerful summer storms sweep in. We didn't have a storm cellar, but we never ended up needing one. I picked out the spots where Marcy's swing set once stood and where my mother had her clothesline. I turned and walked the perimeter of the property,

TWO DREAMS & OTHER TALES
Passing Through

summoning other long-forgotten memories. My trip through this part of my past took about twenty minutes, by which time I was feeling terribly emotional.

When I got back to the car, the sound of gravel crunching under the tires of another vehicle got my attention. I turned and saw a Hillman County police cruiser behind me. The only thing visible in the windshield was the reflected sky. I could not see the occupant, but then I didn't have to. As he stepped out and removed his shades, I thought that the years had been kind to my old teacher. He had become mostly gray up top but was still ruggedly handsome and still had that wide, amiable smile.

He stepped toward me, held out his hand, and spoke in that deep Texas accent of his.

"Hello, Byron. How are you doing, buddy?"

I took his hand and shook it vigorously. "Hello, Mr. Deavers," I said, forcing a smile. "It sure has been a long time."

"Oh please. You're old enough to call me Joe now. So, please do."

"OK, Joe. A little bird told me you made a late career change, but I had to see this to believe it. What made you give up teaching and join the long arm of the law?"

He grinned and said, "Economics. When the bottom fell out of the local economy, everything took a hit, including the schools. When the cuts came, industrial arts were on the chop list, so I got laid off. The sheriff had an opening, and I had been a part-time cop before, so I took the job. It's not my chosen profession, but it's not a terrible life and it pays the bills."

"Did the football program survive?"

He chuckled. "This is Texas, Byron. Football is like religion around here. Of course, it survived."

I chuckled too and asked, "Why do I sense that your presence here is not a coincidence?"

"Because it isn't. That same little bird spoke to me as well."

TWO DREAMS & OTHER TALES
Passing Through

"I guess in your position, having Holly Kendall in your spy network is a useful thing."

"That's for sure. Not much gets past that girl."

"Oh, I don't know about that," I said. "She didn't recognize me until I told her why I was there."

He laughed out loud. "She didn't mention that. That's kind of surprising, though. Besides the fact that you've been in the news lately, that girl was awfully sweet on you in high school."

"So, I heard. I get the impression she still is. I'm assuming she's a married woman, though. I don't know the mysterious Mr. Kendall, do I?"

"No, you wouldn't know him. Besides, he's not around anymore. He died in a motorcycle accident over on Huntington four years ago. He left Holly behind with a baby."

We briefly found ourselves with an awkward silence. Joe had come to me because Holly told him I was in town. She obviously told him about our conversation, so he came to talk. I leaned against the fender of my car and kicked at the gravel beneath my feet. At last, I said, "I was hesitant to call you because I didn't know where we stood."

His expression turned troubled. "Byron, I've always wondered what became of you. I wasn't sure if you stopped getting my letters, or if you just stopped answering them."

"It was the latter and I'm sorry about that," I said. "It wasn't personal, Joe. I simply reached a breaking point. When I went to prison, I still believed it was all a big mistake that would soon get cleared up. One day, about nine months in, I said or did something that set off another inmate and he beat the hell out of me. Two days later, I was still in the infirmary when my legal aid lawyer told me through this fog of pain that my father was dead. I waited several months for word from my mother, but she never wrote or called. I stopped caring after that. Not only didn't I answer my mail anymore, I stopped reading it. I went off to a real dark place and stayed there for a couple of years. Momma would have been appalled at the ugly, profane person I became. Eventually, I pulled out of it simply because all that anger was just too heavy to carry. By then, nobody was trying to stay in contact with me anymore."

Another long, awkward silence ensued. I looked at my right hand and flexed the fingers slowly and deliberately. I said, "Holly told me you might have some answers for me."

He leaned back against the fender of his cruiser as if he were getting comfortable. He crossed his arms and asked, "What would you like to know?"

"What's the buzz around here?"

"The buzz?"

"You know. Byron Welles is innocent, out of prison, and may come back to Hillman. How do people around here feel about all that?"

He hesitated. "That's... that's a tough question. The sense I get is that people are nervous about this. Some are even afraid."

"Why would my coming back here make people nervous? Or afraid?" I was pretty sure I already knew the answer.

"Byron, this entire business was one big travesty. An innocent four-year-old child died in a fire, an innocent eighteen-year-old boy went to prison, and a vicious killer lived comfortably in our midst for fourteen years. Most of the people here had nothing to do with your case, and yet there is a collective guilt. The news coverage has left this community embarrassed. They can't give Donna and Sammy any justice now, and there's no proper way to make it up to you. For a while, at least, your presence is going to make people uncomfortable. Donna Fuller could tell you all about that."

"Well, for what it's worth," I said, with an edge in my voice, "I don't plan on being a presence around here. I'm just passing through." I understood that what he was talking about was basic human nature. However, I also felt that there were at least three victims of this "travesty" repeatedly overlooked. I put that thought aside for the moment.

I let out a slow breath and wiped the perspiration from my forehead. "Tell me about Colin Garver. I haven't seen the depositions yet, so I've never learned what motivated him. Why did he do what he did? What was all of that about, anyway?"

Joe rubbed his eyes and let out a heavy breath before he spoke. "A couple of months before the Oak Terrace fire, right after Darryl Fuller died, Donna had a run-in with Colin. She was walking with her little girl to the drugstore on Main Street. She saw Colin apparently menacing some teenager over something stupid. Others were watching from a distance, but nobody would intervene, so Donna did. She told him he was a brute and should pick on someone his own size. She then led the kid into the drugstore and wouldn't let him leave until Colin was gone. Not even Colin Garver would hit a woman, especially in front of witnesses, but he'd never forget being humiliated by one. The night of the fire, he went over to the Fuller house. It was just after nightfall and the house was dark. He couldn't imagine anyone went to bed that early, so he assumed they weren't home. He decided a little fire damage would teach her a lesson, but he was seriously drunk and the fire got out of control. And you know the rest."

"Unbelievable," I said, shaking my head back and forth. "Why did he choose *me* to take the fall? Why not just disappear into the night and let the identity of the arsonist be a mystery?"

"In this town, who would *you* suspect first? Who would *you* go after first? Colin *was* the first suspect, but he diverted attention from himself by giving the sheriff someone else to pursue. He chose you because everyone was aware of your association with the Fullers. Everyone knew you went there on Tuesdays."

"A target of opportunity," I said with disgust. "Wrong place. Wrong time." I stood up and paced a bit, then turned and pointed at the empty foundations. "So, what was *this* all about? Why did he hurt my family? What did they ever do to him?"

"After the trial," Joe said, "when the town finally calmed down, people started to question the whole business. Some people thought there had been a rush to judgement and that Mr. Marshall might have moved too fast and gotten it wrong. Your mother became a familiar sight at the sheriff's department, the courthouse, and the newspaper, lobbying anyone she could think of to get your case reopened. Her efforts were making Colin nervous, so he tried to scare your folks into leaving town. This time, he made certain nobody was home. He insisted that he never meant for anyone to die, but once again, it got out of hand. Still, your mother left town, so he accomplished that part of his plan."

"Didn't it occur to him that another arson fire—at my house, no less—might cast doubt on my conviction?"

"Nobody ever accused Colin Garver of being smart," he said. "Even if people suspected him, nobody could prove it. So, everybody got over it and moved on."

"Everybody except for Donna Fuller and me," I said, shaking my head. "How did *she* come out of all of this?"

He was quiet for a few seconds, appearing almost sad. "She spent a long time recovering. She never married again or had other children. People see her around town and they see a lone, tragic figure. Everyone's sympathetic, but nobody is sure what to do for her. I spoke with her right after this news broke and do you know what she told me? She was always certain it was Colin. She never forgot the look he gave her that day in front of the drugstore. After the fire, he steered a wide berth around her whenever they crossed paths, like his conscience bothered him or something. She always knew, but couldn't prove it. She wishes she could have for your sake."

There didn't seem to be much else to say on that subject, so Joe and I just looked at the ground for a while. I kicked at the gravel again. Finally, I asked, "What can you tell me about my mother?"

He was quiet for a long time, trying to collect his thoughts. This was important to me, and he wanted to get it right. Finally, he spoke. "Like I said, your mother kept after your case with great determination. I could see it was taking a toll, and I tried to help her as much as I could, but I was not welcome around your father. Given my close friendship with you, he saw me as something of a rival. Mostly, it was my wife, Maureen, who kept up with your mother and helped her whenever she could. You remember Maureen, don't you?"

TWO DREAMS & OTHER TALES
Passing Through

"Of course, a fine lady." I remembered Maureen Deavers well. As a pastor's daughter and a committed believer, her friendship was probably just what Momma needed. I asked, "What can you tell me about the fire?"

"The night of that fire, your folks came home to find the house burning. The fire department came, but it was beyond saving. Then a lot of other people came to help, including Maureen and myself. It was your pastor, Doctor McCollough, who took charge. He made the family life center over at the church available and we all helped them settle in there. An hour later, your mother was frantically calling 911. Your father was having a heart attack or a seizure. They responded quickly, but he died on the way to the hospital."

Joe paused, and I was glad that he did. I'd never heard this before and needed a moment to digest it. In my mind's eye, I could still clearly see Daddy there on the courthouse steps the day they took me away. I couldn't forget the hurt I caused him that day and the guilt I still carried because of it. I resumed my place against the car fender, lowered my head into my hands, and rubbed my eyes.

Finally, he continued. "When we saw her the next morning, your mother looked awful. She was clinging to Marcy, who wouldn't stop crying about her daddy. Maureen took Marcy aside, and I sat down with your mother. She had little money and there was no insurance from the house, so I told her I would take care of the arrangements. I'll never forget how she responded. Those shattered eyes turned hard, and she said, 'Joseph, I can't thank you and Maureen enough for all you've done for us. But I have no intention of burying my husband in the town that murdered him and destroyed my boy. I'm leaving this place and taking my husband with me.' I wasn't sure what she meant by that, but I took the hint and backed off. It was Doctor McCollough who helped her place your father in a church yard over in Jenkinsville. I can give you the address—"

"I know where it is," I said abruptly, interrupting him. "I was there earlier today." I held up my hand and lowered my eyes. "Sorry. That was rude."

He just shook his head. "No, that's OK. There was no funeral. Just a burial service. There were eight of us there that day. Doctor McCollough and the other pastor presided. There was also your mother, Marcy, Maureen, me, and two of your classmates."

"Don't tell me. Danny Bell and Holly Richards?"

"In the flesh. They came together. Danny was home on leave from the Army before going to his new posting overseas. He came in his dress uniform. Your mother cried in his arms."

This didn't surprise me. Danny was my best friend from sixth grade on and he spent a lot of time at our house. He lost his mother at an early age and I gladly shared mine with him—and my mother really liked him. As for Holly, I had discovered over the last hour she was apparently my other best friend. Like a typical teenage boy, I was too oblivious to catch on. I should have taken that girl to the senior prom.

"After the service," Joe said, "I followed your mother's beat-up old car out of the church parking lot. Instead of turning left and coming back here to Hillman, she turned right and headed west. I never saw her again."

I suddenly had this mental image of my mother driving her car off the end of the earth into oblivion. I shook my head to dispel it. "Where do you think she went?"

"I think the only place she wanted to be was where you were. Obviously, she never got there." He thought for a moment. "If I had to speculate, I would guess that she drove that car as far as it would go. When the tank was empty and she had no more money, she might have sold it for bus fare or a place to stay while she planned her next move."

I lowered my head and closed my eyes, imagining how desperate and distraught Momma must have been. But what became of her and Marcy? It was like the earth opened and swallowed them whole, leaving no clues behind.

"Do you think she's still alive?" I asked. He opened his mouth to speak, but I threw up my hand and spoke first. "No, don't answer that. It's not fair of me to ask. Besides, I believe I already know."

Joe looked at me expectantly. "She didn't live long after she left here," I said. "I have nothing to base that on except her silence. Even if she didn't come to me, she would have contacted me somehow. She would have wanted to be the one to tell me about Daddy. She wouldn't have cut me off completely and stayed in hiding all these years. The problem is that my lawyer has found no death certificate for Momma anywhere in the state of Texas. That gives me hope, at least. If she's dead, she's most likely a Jane Doe in some potter's field somewhere. But that leaves the question of whatever became of my little sister. The child protection system has no record of her or anyone fitting her details. Is it possible that someone might have taken her in without going through legal channels?"

"It's possible," Joe said. "It's not legal, but I'm sure it's happened before. My wife works in social services. If you'd like, I'll get her to look into this some more for you."

"I would appreciate that. Tell me. If you were going to search for them, how would you go about it?"

He thought about that for a bit. "I'd get pictures of your mother and Marcy, if you have any, and have the one of Marcy age-enhanced. I can arrange that for you. Then, I'd get a map, locate the bus routes, and just start driving. I'd hit all the small towns, show people the pictures, and ask a lot of questions. Somebody somewhere might remember them. Perhaps I'd get an investigator to do it all for me. I can probably find one for you."

"You realize that two of those *small towns* are Dallas and Fort Worth, don't you?" I asked. "Big cities are easy to get lost in. I'm looking for a needle in a haystack here and I'm not even sure how big the haystack is. If you were me, would you undertake this?"

"Absolutely," he said without hesitation. He rose from his resting place against the cruiser. "If my wife, one of my girls, or one of my sisters were missing, I would never stop looking for them. Family is everything."

I nodded agreement. There was no question about proceeding with this quest, but I had to get free of my current legal restraints first. Still, the trail was cold, and it was going to be a long, grueling process. I had to be prepared for the possibility that I might never find the answers I wanted. I stood up once again and walked across the driveway into the side yard. I stopped and stood there, silently staring into space for a while, reviewing in my mind all the things we'd been discussing.

Joe stepped up behind me and broke into my thoughts. "What else would you like to talk about, Byron?"

"I think I'm good for now."

He was silent for a moment, then said, "I remember when you used to come to me with your problems. You'd come into my classroom after school like you were just there to hang out. You'd pace the floor, wring your hands, and fidget. When you were finally ready to tell me what was bothering you, we'd talk about it until we were both late for dinner. You haven't changed. We've been talking about a lot of difficult things here. Yet, no matter how much ground we cover, you keep right on pacing, wiping your brow, kicking the gravel, shaking your head, and so on. Something else is clearly on your mind. Talk to me."

There *was* more on my mind, but I hesitated to broach it, fearing I might say something I'd regret. I turned and looked to see him with his arms crossed and a look of expectation. He knew if he waited long enough, I'd speak. He'd always won this waiting game before, and this time would be no different.

"Momma insisted that we be a church-going, God-fearing family," I said. "You know, of course, that we attended First Baptist, where Doc McCollough was pastor. When I was twelve, a new kid joined the youth group, and we immediately disliked each other. I'm not sure why. One day, our rivalry got out of hand and we got into one hell of a fight. Doc got us both by the collar, dragged us into his study, and gave us a stern lecture. He told us young Christian men were supposed to set a better example, and he talked at length about why forgiveness was so important. I tell you it wasn't just platitudes with him, either. He then put us in the family life center and told us we would not be leaving there until we forgave each other for our appalling behavior." I laughed out loud. "We didn't come out until the next morning. Boy, was my mother angry."

Joe smiled. "That other kid was Danny Bell, wasn't it?"

TWO DREAMS & OTHER TALES
Passing Through

"Yes, it was. From that day on, we were best friends, practically brothers. We stayed that way until the summer he joined the Army, and I went to prison. I never forgot the lesson I learned that night about forgiveness. At least, not until the day I took that beating. That's when I tossed my faith aside and swore that I would never forgive the unnamed person who put me in that place."

I took a deep breath and continued. "When I heard that Colin Garver confessed and was being counseled by the pastor of my former church, I changed my tune. I told myself that for my mother's sake I would forgive him, but only after he told me himself why he hurt me and my family; only if he convinced me of his remorse. I really needed to have that conversation with him, but it never took place. I blame Ed Chandler for that."

"I don't understand. Why do you blame Chandler?"

I searched for the right words before continuing. "Joe, most of what I know about Colin's situation I got from the news. The rest is speculation on my part. From what I heard and what I understand of Baptist preachers, Chandler did what a good pastor is supposed to do. He counseled him on the wages of sin, the need to confess and repent, the need to pray for salvation, and in this case, seek forgiveness from his victims. I have no reason to believe Pastor Ed was untruthful about that part of the story. I truly hope Colin found salvation. After fourteen years of hell on earth, I wouldn't wish the real thing on my worst enemy. Anyway, after that, Chandler convinced Colin that it was time to square things with the law. You were there, so I'm sure you know how that played out."

"Of course. He came into the sheriff's office with Chandler and a lawyer named Aaron Denby and made a full confession to the sheriff and one of our detectives. We had a real gray area there because the case had been closed for years with a successful conviction and the new suspect was dying. The sheriff called the local district court judge, who ordered Colin held overnight and for the prosecutor's office to get on it. The sheriff was told to keep the whole thing under wraps for the time being, as if that were even possible. It was mighty awkward jailing Colin in his condition. The next morning, the prosecutor, Mr. Marshall, ordered us to bring him to the courthouse. He gave his confession in a sworn deposition that took all morning. The judge then ordered him released on his own recognizance."

"I suppose I should be grateful to Ed Chandler for all of that," I said. "It's the reason I'm almost in the clear now. What I have a problem with is what happened next. Do you remember what Colin, Chandler, and the lawyer found outside the courthouse that day?"

"A sea of reporters," Joe said, rolling his eyes.

"A sea of reporters," I repeated. "And who arranged that?"

"Nobody seems to know. Neither the sheriff nor the prosecutor released the story, so someone must have leaked it."

"Someone leaked it?" I asked dubiously. "Less than eighteen hours after Colin makes a non-public confession, you have a spontaneous gathering of reporters from all over East Texas on the courthouse lawn? That's a mighty big leak. You think maybe somebody made a lot of phone calls and passed the word to embarrass someone or keep it from getting swept under the rug?"

"You sound just like the sheriff," he said with a grin. "He thinks the same thing and would like to have a long talk with whoever did it. I can't say I blame him, though I'm certainly glad you're getting a fair hearing now. Sometimes justice needs a push."

I stared at Joe for a moment, but he said nothing more. He either had a great poker face or honestly did not know who my unidentified supporter was. Rather than pursue that, I said, "It was breaking news on television that day and what a circus that was. The leaker clearly wasn't Colin's lawyer. The only thing he could think of to say was 'no comment.' Then Chandler jumps in and turns the whole thing into an impromptu revival meeting. He tells them all how this poor misguided soul fell victim to the evil influence of alcohol and committed a desperate crime which shocked the community; how he lived for years with the guilt of that crime; how God finally dealt with him and showed him mercy; and how Colin had come forward to do the right thing for the victims and accept the consequences of his actions.

TWO DREAMS & OTHER TALES
Passing Through

"It was a very inspiring story, but mostly inaccurate. First, Colin was not some poor soul who took an unexpected detour over to the dark side one night. He was evil his whole miserable life. He was also dying, so he wouldn't live long enough to face any consequences. And the so-called desperate crime was not a single act. He burned down *two* houses, killed *two* people, and destroyed *two* families. It really annoys me how many people see all this in the news and still don't seem to understand I once had a family, too."

I took a deep breath to steady myself, then continued. "Chandler tried to get Colin to say a few words and perhaps answer questions, but Colin wouldn't speak. According to the press, he went home and never spoke or appeared in public again. Those of us who were still waiting to hear from him were out of luck. Why? My guess is that having a microphone put in his face was never part of his plan. He was just a poor, dying sinner who wanted to say he was sorry, not become a media spectacle. He was probably humiliated that day.

"Three days after I got out of prison, I saw on the TV news where Colin Garver, the self-confessed killer from Hillman County, was laid to rest that day. They showed a clip of the burial and I couldn't believe the size of the crowd there to pay their respects, like he was some kind of fallen hero. That's when this loud voice began shouting in my head. 'What about us? What about George and Patty and Marcy and Byron? What about the Welles family? Where's *our* apology? Where's *our* plea for forgiveness and understanding? Where's *our* justice? Where's *our* outpouring of community support? Where's *our* redemption?'"

By this point, I was shouting. As my deep-seated anger came flooding out into the open, Joe's eyes got wider. He said, "Byron, I didn't realize how bad it was for you. You're angry about this, aren't you?"

I exploded, "You're damned right I'm angry!! If Doc McCollough were here, he'd tell me I was being selfish! He'd come up with the words to put me in the right frame of mind! But he's not here and I don't know how to get there on my own! Selfish is the only way I know how to be right now! When Colin burned down these houses, he burned down my life! I want that life back, Joe! I want to be whole again, and to know that there are more than just three people in this lousy, stinking town who give a damn!" I took several deep breaths, trying to bring myself back under control. Pointing at the empty foundation of my house, I said quietly, "I just want to come home to my family, Joe. I want things like they were. Is that so much to ask?"

My lip quivered, my hands shook, and my eyes welled up. Suddenly weak in the knees, I was on the verge of falling down, so Joe Deavers stepped forward and pulled me into a firm embrace. At that moment, the floodgates opened, and I cried harder than I'd ever cried in my life. There was a lot of anger and frustration in those tears, but mostly it was grief; grief over the loss of Samantha Fuller, my family, my home, and fourteen years of my life to a series of senseless acts committed by a drunken bully.

As I stood there in my old teacher's arms, I felt very safe and very foolish at the same time. I couldn't say how long we stayed like that, but when I finally brought myself under control, I pulled away from him. As he watched, I furiously wiped my eyes as though I were trying to cover up the evidence of my momentary weakness. I could only think of one way to break the stress and tension of the moment, so I looked at him and said, "You never did *that* in shop class."

Joe laughed hard. When he caught his breath, he said, "If I had, I probably would have lost my job."

"In that case, you're fired," I said. Then we both laughed.

When the humor passed, he became serious again. "Byron, you *are* going to be whole again. You need to believe that."

"Why, Joe?" I asked, still wiping my eyes. "Why do I need to believe that?"

He shook his head back and forth and said, "Because life is too long a journey to make without hope. You need to believe in something."

"I've forgotten how to believe, Joe. I don't even remember how to pray."

"You could learn a thing or two from my wife. She prays more than any three other people I know."

TWO DREAMS & OTHER TALES
Passing Through

"Does it help?"

He thought about that, then said, "Sometimes it does."

"Would you ask her to pray for me?"

"She already does, Byron. She always has." That didn't surprise me. "As for your wish to find more people in this town who care, I can give you number four: Donna Fuller." I looked at him questioningly. "The day I spoke to her, she asked that if I saw you, would I please send you her way? She really wants to see you."

"I don't know, Joe. That would be mighty awkward. I'm not sure I could face her."

"Why not, Byron?" He sounded almost annoyed. "You didn't hurt her or Sammy. You were their friend."

"I wasn't that much of a friend."

"You don't think so? She told me they both enjoyed your visits when you came with the groceries. You were pleasant and respectful, and Donna found that very refreshing. She really appreciated how you took the time to visit with her little girl. Sammy was shy and didn't have many friends. She'd recently lost her daddy and was still in turmoil over it. She reveled in the attention you gave her and once told her mother that she couldn't wait until she was old enough to be your girlfriend."

"Oh, for Pete's sake, Joe," I said, impatiently. "I don't need to hear that."

"Yes, you do!" he practically shouted. "Yes, you do. Don't you get it, Byron? You say you want to be whole again. The way you do that is by reconnecting with people. Here you have an old friend reaching out to you, so reach back. Go visit her, have coffee with her, and let her tell you that story herself. Cry on each other's shoulders if you need to. While you're at it, call Holly Kendall and fix up a lunch date. Danny Bell is back in the area, so give him a ring. Pick a night and come join Maureen and me for dinner. That's how you do it, Byron. Just reach out."

TWO DREAMS & OTHER TALES
Passing Through

"What if I decide I don't want to come back to this town?" I asked defiantly.

"Then don't. That doesn't mean you can't have friends here."

I stared at him for a long time and finally realized he was right. Before I set out that day, I'd told myself I could not be truly free until I returned to the place where my freedom was first taken from me. That was why I came to town with no agenda except to make a pointless inquiry at the post office, an inquiry I could have made by phone. Joe was making a similar point. I had spent my whole previous life in this town, so I had no other point of reference. For me, the long road back needed to begin here with people I knew and loved.

"I'll tell you what, Joe," I said. "If you give me the address and make the call, I'll go by and see Miss Donna on my way out."

"Good," he said with a broad smile. "Very good."

He pulled a leather cardholder from his pocket, reached into it, and came out with a small white card. He scribbled on it, then handed it to me. I read the address and recognized the street name. I turned the card over and saw the county's coat of arms on the left edge. In the middle were the words: *Sgt. Joseph K. Deavers, Hillman County Sheriff's Office*. The bottom right corner had a phone number and an email address listed.

"That's my cell number," he said. "Use it whenever you need it. I can make official inquiries for you or just discuss ideas with you. Or if you feel the need to chat about nothing in particular, just pick up the phone. I'm always here."

It was my second offer of renewed friendship that day. I'd forgotten what having friends was like, so for a moment, I felt overwhelmed. Finally, I said, "You and Holly really turned it around for me today, Joe. I can't thank you enough." He reached out his hand as he'd done when he arrived, and I shook it vigorously once again.

He turned and walked back to the cruiser. As he opened the door, he looked back. "One more thing," he said. "You can't get closure from Colin Garver, but there's nothing to prevent you from visiting Ed Chandler and telling him what you told me. He's actually a pretty good guy. Who knows? He may find what you have to say useful." I gave him a long, hard stare. He grinned and said, "Just something to think about."

He climbed into the cruiser, pulled out his cell phone, and spoke into it for a moment. Finally, he opened his window and spoke. "She's home and expecting you. Good luck."

"Thanks, Joe." A moment later, I was watching him drive back toward town.

I walked to my car and opened the door. Before climbing in, I took one last long look around the property. I told Joe that I wanted to come home, but I realized the elements that made this place home had long since fled. Even if I did eventually move back to Hillman, I couldn't imagine ever coming here again. I got into the car, started it, and backed out of the driveway. As I drove down Berry Hollow Road, my childhood home slowly passed from sight.

***

Dallas, Texas
6 August 2013

Dear Momma,

I'm sure there are those who will think it odd that I'm writing a letter I can't mail to a mother who might not even be living. My reason is that I am very lonely this evening and want nothing more than to have a long talk with my mother. It's been so many years since we last spoke. My hope is that this letter will eventually find you and May-May alive and well. My greatest desire, however, is that one day we will all be together again. As a dear friend told me, just today, family is everything.

First, I have news for you. I'm going to be a free man soon. A man from Hillman recently confessed on his deathbed to the crimes I went to prison for. He was also the one who hurt our family by burning our house. He confessed because he did not want to meet God with a guilty conscience. My lawyer got me released from prison and assures me they will soon overturn my conviction. I know you would wish for my sake that I forgive the man who did all of this. I'm trying my best to do so.

Second, I visited Daddy's grave for the first time today. You picked a pleasant spot. It's peaceful and has a wonderful view. It's a good place to think and remember, and I did so for nearly an hour. Daddy and I always had a bit of a strained relationship, but I never doubted that he loved me. I'm sure he believed I loved him, too. I have missed you both so much over the years.

I also visited Hillman today. The place still looks much the same as I remember it. I spoke with Joe Deavers. Do you remember him? He told me about your last days there and I can't tell you how much it pains me to learn about your difficulties. I understand why you had to leave, though I wish I knew where you and May-May went. God willing, I will find both of you.

Momma, I'm not sure what to say about my prison years. I lost my way for a long time and became someone I'm not proud of. Perhaps in time, I will rediscover my faith and become whole again. I can't say for sure what the future holds. I haven't been out long enough to plan. When I got my college acceptance, I promised you and Daddy that I would make you proud of me. That promise still holds. It's strange that at thirty-two, I'm trying to decide what I'll do when I grow up. Whatever I end up doing, I will do my best to bring honor back to our family name.

There's not a lot I can say about my present circumstance. I had no family available to take me in, so they placed me in this halfway house here in Dallas. They run a tight ship here. Lights are out in a few minutes, so I'll close for now. Until I see you again, I am your loyal, loving, and devoted son.

George Byron Welles, Jr.

***

Texas, December 2014

I stood at my parent's grave with mixed feelings. Sixteen months earlier, I promised my father that the next time I came, I would bring my mother. I didn't know if she would be coming to visit or to stay. To my dismay, it turned out to be the latter.

The first few months of my search had been very difficult. I covered most of the same ground my lawyer had and learned nothing new. Maureen Deavers then suggested to me that restricting my search to Texas was shortsighted, given the proximity of Hillman to three other states—Louisiana, Arkansas, and Oklahoma. She spent several months making inquiries of the child welfare agencies of those states, and finally struck gold. The search turned up a female adoptee of unknown origin—her name was Marcy Whitfield—who was now a college student at the University of Oklahoma. It didn't take long to confirm she was my sister.

I pieced together most of the story from official reports. Two months after leaving Hillman, my mother and sister rode into a small Oklahoma town aboard a bus. Momma had almost no money left and no identification on her. Marcy was found sleeping by her side, sadly unaware that her mother had quietly passed away. The official ruling for my mother's death was "natural causes," though I suspect grief, fear, and extreme anxiety overwhelmed her already fragile health. Unable to tell anything about herself apart from her first name, my sister became a ward of the state and was eventually adopted by an older couple from Tulsa. I have never figured out how or why my family ended up in Oklahoma.

The important thing was that I now knew Momma and Daddy were resting together in the arms of God. It had been less than a week since Momma's reinterment. When Daddy died, she had not had the time or money to place a proper grave marker over him, so Dr. McCollough and his church arranged it for her. He made certain her name was on the stone next to Daddy's, even though it was unclear if she would ever be laid to rest there.

I had put off coming until Marcy could come with me. We stood hand in hand, looking down at the marker. The pain of losing my mother was made a lot easier to bear by having my baby sister back in my life. She had grown into a beautiful, confident young woman and I couldn't have been prouder. Our reunion was awkward because, though she remembered me, the memories were vague as memories of early childhood often are.

TWO DREAMS & OTHER TALES
Passing Through

She'd always known, at least, that her parents were in heaven and that the brother she only remembered as "By-By" was out there somewhere.

What might have seemed unusual to anyone passing by was our appearance. Beneath her overcoat, my sister was wearing a flowing pink dress that started with a high collar and fell almost to her ankles. She wore my mother's cameo at her throat and a small corsage of bright-colored flowers pinned to the lapel of her coat. Her long red hair sat atop her head in a stylish weave. I was in a black tuxedo with a ruffled white shirt, a black bow tie with long tails, and a red cummerbund. No doubt our wedding attire looked out of place in a cemetery.

Marcy asked, "Do you think Momma and Daddy are happy to be together again?"

"I think they've been together all along," I said, "but I'm sure they're thrilled we found one another."

"I just wish I could remember them better. It would be nice to remember the important things."

I released her hand, put my arm around her shoulder, and drew her in close. "The most important thing for you to remember is that they loved you more than life itself. In case I haven't told you already, I love you too. I hope you never get tired of hearing me say it."

"No chance of that, big brother. I waited an awful long time to hear you say it."

I looked at my watch. "We need to get on over to Hillman now. There's somebody over there who waited a long time to hear me say it, too."

***

Hillman Weekly News
December 11, 2014

KENDALL—WELLES

Holly Jane Kendall and George Byron Welles wed last Saturday in a private ceremony at Plainfield United Methodist Church in Hillman County. The Rev. Donald Harris officiated.

TWO DREAMS & OTHER TALES
Passing Through

The bride is the daughter of Mr. & Mrs. Andrew H. Richards of Hillman. She is a 1999 graduate of Hillman High School and has been employed by the United States Postal Service since 2002. She is a lifelong member of Plainfield UMC, past president of the Hillman Rescue Squad Ladies Auxiliary, and the mother of a six-year-old son, David Kendall, Jr.

The groom is the son of the late Mr. & Mrs. George B. Welles, Sr., formerly of Hillman. He is a 1999 graduate of Hillman High School and is currently a student at Texas Tech University. He is also a part-time employee of Spencer & Associates, an engineering firm in Lubbock.

The bride's maid of honor was her sister, Mrs. Suzanne Sadler, of San Antonio. The best man was Staff Sgt. Daniel J. Bell (former U.S. Army) of Hillman County. Both were accompanied by their respective spouses, Mr. Joshua Sadler, and Mrs. Sarah Bell. The bride was given away by her parents.

Also in attendance were Miss Marcy Whitfield, of Norman, Oklahoma, sister of the groom; Mrs. Donna Fuller of Hillman; Sgt. & Mrs. Joseph Deavers of Hillman; and Rev. Dr. Jonathan D. McCollough of Fort Worth.

The groom dedicated the occasion to the memory of his parents.

After a short honeymoon, Mr. & Mrs. Welles and their son will make their home in Lubbock.

TWO DREAMS & OTHER TALES
Passing Through

Tale #2. Two Dreams

The First Dream
Atlanta, 1955–1999

As far back as I can remember, my father was a dreamer. Though grateful for the good things that came his way, he never stopped setting new goals and devising plans to reach them. I've often thought he would have loved climbing mountains, if he knew how, at least until he conquered Everest. In the business world, they call people like him "entrepreneurs." I like the word "dreamer" better. While Dad doggedly pursued many challenges in his lifetime, two particular dreams meant more to him than any other. The first was born in the most unlikely of places.

For eight years, my father served in the US Army as a cook. In the military, this is not a profession that gains one a lot of glory, but as Napoleon once said, an army marches on its stomach. If you don't feed the troops, they don't fight. So, my father and his colleagues were important players in a very important enterprise. Though America saw no significant combat during those years, Dad still learned a lot about the logistics of providing rations to fighting men in the field. His primary education, however, was learning how an Army mess hall operates. One commonly hears about privates peeling potatoes and servers dishing out "mystery meat" and other unappetizing fare on a serving line, but that is mostly stereotype. My father and his mates learned the basics of supply and requisition, dietary and nutritional requirements, balanced menu planning, preparing and serving meals for large numbers of men and women, and maintaining a clean and sanitary facility. He took great pride in doing the job well and respected the non-comms who devoted entire careers to this calling. Amidst all that, Dad discovered his first glorious dream. He looked forward to post-military life when he planned on being the proprietor of a hugely popular fine dining establishment where everyone knew and respected the name Thomas Kemp.

When Dad mustered out of the Army in 1963, he hit the ground running. Within a year and a half, he had married his longtime sweetheart, Alice Pennington, and fathered his first and only child—my name is Noah.

TWO DREAMS & OTHER TALES
Two Dreams

My father lost both of his parents while he was in the Army and his only sibling, an estranged sister, lived on the West Coast. That made Mom and me his only close family. My parents had known each other as children in Atlanta and became reacquainted when Dad was stationed at Fort Benning. Not wanting to drag her around the country with him, he decided to finish his second hitch, return to civilian life, and then marry her. As part of his plea for her hand, he shared his dream with her so she would know he had prospects.

It was a couple of months before my birth when my father opened his small restaurant. It was July 1964, and he called his new place The Crossroads. The name was geographical, as the restaurant sat at the intersection of Stratford and Claymore Avenues on the outskirts of Atlanta. While these were well-traveled thoroughfares, the real estate in that area was undeveloped both commercially and residentially. To a businessman thinking in the short term, this wouldn't seem like a suitable location for a restaurant, at least not if one wanted it to succeed. However, my father rarely thought in the short term. He foresaw the day when the ever-expanding local business district would move down Stratford Avenue, past that intersection and out to the suburbs. He pictured a much larger restaurant dominating that crossroad which, by then, would be the focal point of the neighborhood. For this reason, he bought a much bigger lot than he needed at the time—at a dirt-cheap price.

In a city with plenty of opportunities for fine dining, luring patrons out to the suburbs for dinner required a restaurant with something special. It needed a business model that promoted long and steady growth, and an ambitious marketing plan. Once the business opened, it needed to sell itself by word of mouth. Some of the best advertising a restaurant can get is the enthusiastic recommendation of a satisfied customer. An impressed food critic or two doesn't hurt either.

There was one business model that appealed to my father. Dad was impressed with the staying power of family-owned and operated businesses, whether large or small. No matter the social dynamic in a business family, they have a vested interest in one another's success and act accordingly. Dad didn't have enough family to operate that type of business, so he created his

TWO DREAMS & OTHER TALES
Two Dreams

own family business concept. He made a family of his workers, stressing the notion that they take care of one another while the boss takes care of them all. Even part time and short-term employees came under the family umbrella.

Before every opening, he would make the rounds and inspect the troops. He would attempt to talk to employees, showing an interest in what they were working on and even how they were doing personally. He never pried, but he made a point through conversation and frequent social occasions to get to know employees and their families. He made himself available when they had special needs. He always said the personal touch made for a more productive workforce. To add to that productivity, my father hired the best he could find in several specialties and used these experts to teach and train their less experienced colleagues. All the employees loved and respected my dad. Over the years, it had become their tradition to call him Mr. K, a casual nickname that still imparted respect.

On the customer side, patrons were treated like visiting royalty at The Crossroads. Dad worked the room when other responsibilities didn't tie him down. He would welcome the patrons, solicit comments on the service, and engage in conversation. In this way, he came to be on a first-name basis with many of them. By getting to know the likes and dislikes of the regular patrons, he and his staff could anticipate their wants and wishes. Few things will impress a customer—or a food critic—more than attentiveness to such details. As Dad always said, a satisfied customer is a repeat customer.

This approach to business, along with his various efforts to support civic organizations and events, earned him and his restaurant a lot of goodwill in the community. Competitors came and went, but The Crossroads kept going; as long as my father did, anyway. The accurate test of his staying power would be the ability of the business to continue after he retired from it. Dad's thoughts on that subject gave birth to his second glorious dream: that I would one day succeed him.

My mother accepted early on that my father had a mistress—his restaurant—and another family by her, but she never doubted his devotion to his own family. Dad had three hard and fast rules that kept that devotion strong. The first was that the business did not open on Sunday, a day

TWO DREAMS & OTHER TALES
Two Dreams

reserved for God and family. The Kemps always spent that day together. The second was that Dad took one night off each week—almost always Thursday—leaving the business in the capable hands of his floor manager. One place my parents never spent their date night was at The Crossroads. The last rule was that we left town and took a week of family vacation at the end of every summer.

Mom filled up the missed time with Dad by pursuing a career of her own. She loved photography and started a portrait business, working both in her studio and at special events like weddings. Still, it truly was a love story for her and Dad. When she was stricken with ovarian cancer in 1988, we were both by her side every step of the way. When she died, my father was inconsolable, and I didn't do so well myself. He tried to fill the void in his life with work, but ultimately, he found the void was still there. Three years after Mom's passing, he married Joanne Hellman, who was a widow and a longtime patron of The Crossroads. I was living away from home by then and did not get to know her very well at first. Still, she made Dad happy, and that pleased me.

As for Dad and me, we alternated between being very close and somewhat distant. When I was a child, I worshipped him and he doted on me. There were many occasions when he brought me to the restaurant so I could see how everything worked. Inevitably, he would quote that old visionary promise that this would all be mine one day. As a teenager, I worked during summers at the restaurant, partly to save for college, but also to be around my dad. Unfortunately for him, I didn't fall in with his plans for me to succeed him. This wasn't the career I wanted for myself. I attended college, got my degree in finance, and began a career in the financial services field. I made a lot of money for others and for myself as a stockbroker and registered financial planner with a highly respected national firm. Four years into that career, I married my college sweetheart, then pulled up stakes and followed her to North Carolina. I lived away from home throughout the nineties, my connection to Dad becoming more tenuous with each passing year. Despite that, he never gave up on his second dream and his belief that I would one day embrace it as well.

TWO DREAMS & OTHER TALES
Two Dreams

Everything changed in January 1999. Two weeks after Christmas, my sixty-three-year-old father had a massive heart attack. It happened in the main dining room one night during the dinner shift. I rushed home to Atlanta and spent several days keeping vigil while he lingered between life and death. Joanne and I spent those days by his side, holding hands, praying together, and becoming fast friends. Dad survived and a quintuple bypass put him back on his feet, but he never fully recovered. From that point on, he was living on borrowed time. Two things became obvious. The first was that he had to retire. Not only could he not return to his business, but given his driven nature, it wasn't even a good idea for him to remain in the same city. He and Joanne made plans to move to Miami. The second issue was the business itself, which had been closed. Dad's ongoing medical expenses were going to be significant and he wouldn't be able to manage them without access to the equity he had in the business. That meant The Crossroads would have to be sold. It crushed my father to give up his second dream after holding it so closely for thirty-five years.

I had only been back home in Charlotte for two days when everything changed yet again. I awoke one morning to the realization that my father's dream wasn't dead. Twelve years in the financial sector had given me the business savvy and the financial resources to buy my father out if I so chose. I realized I wanted to do it, not just for my father, but for myself. It was like hearing a religious calling and knowing without question what I needed to do.

With my wife's blessing and encouragement, I headed back to Atlanta and had a long, heartfelt talk with my father. He was both happy and disappointed at the same time. He wanted me to keep The Crossroads in the family, but he didn't want me to have to buy my inheritance from him. I finally put it in terms he could accept. I told him I had inherited the most important things from him: his values, his strength, his vision, his love for people, and all the other intangibles that would equip me to do his job. As for finances and training, I told him that God had foreseen the need and that my education and my career had all been part of a divine plan to prepare me for this day. I can't say with certainty I believed that at the time, but I eventually convinced myself. With a rush of emotion, my father gratefully

TWO DREAMS & OTHER TALES
Two Dreams

accepted my proposal, and I became the new prospective owner of The Crossroads.

My next stop was the home of Charlie Magruder, a tall African-American man with a big and solid frame. Despite his very imposing appearance, I thought of him as a gentle giant, a man with a heart of gold and as devoted a friend as one could have. My father would attest to this, as Charlie had become his best friend over the years. At The Crossroads, he had worked his way up from part time bus boy to floor manager, which he had been for sixteen years. He supervised the department heads—executive chef, maître d', operations—and handled many administrative details that couldn't wait for my father's personal attention. On Dad's weekly night off and during his annual vacation, Charlie was the boss. At home, he was a devoted husband and father with a wife he worshipped and a son and daughter he worked hard to put through college.

I shared my vision with Charlie and asked him to help me put The Crossroads back on its feet. He readily agreed. We then rolled up our sleeves and got down to business. I used my contacts and professional skills to arrange financing with a major Atlanta bank and tossed in most of my own capital to make the sale happen. I dealt with all the legal and bureaucratic details needed to put the business into operation again. I also reestablished our relationships with many of the vendors that were dropped without warning when The Crossroads unexpectedly closed its doors. Charlie got to work on personnel matters. He contacted the eighty-four other family members who had suddenly become unemployed in January—that had weighed heavily on Dad's conscience. Charlie managed to rehire fifty-one of them. He then got busy hiring new personnel.

The uninitiated would probably think it was simply a matter of reopening the building and making a few phone calls to get the business moving again. In fact, the entire process took us five months. As we approached the end of our quest, we discussed the date of opening night. The summer was just beginning, and we agreed we would prefer to wait until after the big holiday—Independence Day—and not open on a weekend, which would be busy enough without all the hoopla. We finally came up with our day and let the world know through newspaper ads,

TWO DREAMS & OTHER TALES
Two Dreams

posters, flyers, and word of mouth that The Crossroads would reopen for the dinner shift on Tuesday, July 7.

The Second Dream
Atlanta, July 1999

I was driving east on Stratford Avenue. It was Tuesday, the clock on the dashboard read 3:14 p.m., and the grand reopening of The Crossroads was less than two hours away. This would mark the end of a long journey for Charlie Magruder and me. I'd spent much of the day attending to the last remaining details by visiting our bank, our accountant, our attorney, and one of the licensing agencies that issue our permits.

The weather that day was sunny and very warm; a typical Georgia summer day. I noted the extensive activity along Stratford, including businesses and dwellings of every type, both big and small. Thirty-five years earlier, that stretch of road had been barren. My dad had foreseen the growth and how it would impact his business. In the early years, The Crossroads only served dinner, opening at 3:00 p.m. and closing at 11:00 p.m. Businesses and homes began springing up in large numbers nearby and the local eateries became popular lunchtime destinations. The Crossroads switched to two shifts: lunch from 11:00 a.m. to 3:00 p.m. and dinner from 5:00 p.m. to 11:00 p.m. Between the shifts, he switched out the crews and the menus, restocked the shelves, and began preparing much of what would be served that night.

There was one tradition that never changed, though. Ten minutes before the dinner shift opened, the family of workers would always assemble for what my father called a "muster," a word he first learned in the army. He would take this occasion to tell them he believed in all of them and supported them. He would encourage them to accomplish great things and express his confidence in their ability to do so. Making this daily speech was one of the many tasks I was taking over as the new boss.

The problem was that I wasn't feeling that confident. My unease had started one morning a few days earlier while I was shaving. Looking in the mirror, I saw staring back at me a man who had bet everything he had—including his marriage and his life savings—on a venture he had never even attempted before. It occurred to me that if I failed, a lot of other people would fail with me, some of them landing pretty hard. I asked myself aloud, "What on earth have you done?" During those few days, this sudden panic attack—if I may call it that—only deepened. I knew I had to work my way past it because pessimism is contagious and can become a self-fulfilling prophecy.

As I came around a bend in the road, The Crossroads came into view. A line of trees along the street obscured most of the building, but the big red and white sign was fully visible. It read:

**CROSSROADS FAMILY RESTAURANT
Fine Dining Since 1964**

There was other information written on the sign in smaller print, including the name of the proprietor, Thomas J. Kemp. I hadn't been able to bring myself to paint over my father's name and put my own in its place. I knew I would have to, eventually. Until then, I would leave this bit of false advertising in place and ride on my father's coattails.

As I sat in the left turn lane waiting for a line of cars to pass, I looked over my father's former domain with great admiration. The building and the parking lot had been expanded three times since the original construction. In fact, the building looked nothing like the original. We now had two large dining rooms and enough seating for 180 people at one time. The ceilings were high and the tall windows allowed for a great deal of natural lighting in the daytime and early evening. The kitchen and related facilities were spacious and modernized. Our business was not only very customer-friendly, but state-of-the-art. My father had invested a lot to make it so, and he had the success to show for it. Though I had laid out a lot of my own hard-earned capital to take over my father's legacy, there were those to whom I would still have to prove myself. In recent days, I had become one of my own skeptics.

I pulled around behind the building and into my reserved parking space. Normally, I would unlock the back door and enter through it, but the loading dock was open, so I climbed the steps and entered through there. Many boxes were stacked on the platform and two young men—Kenny and Jeff—were loading them onto a moving cart.

TWO DREAMS & OTHER TALES
Two Dreams

"Good afternoon, fellas."

They saw me for the first time and came to attention. Kenny said, "Hello, Mr. Kemp. Is there something we can do for you?"

"No, I'm good. Sorry to interrupt." I headed for the door, but stopped, turned back, and asked, "Has Mr. Magruder been through here?" The supplier who brought that haul had clearly just been there, so I assumed Charlie had signed for it.

Pointing toward the kitchen entrance, Jeff said, "He headed in that direction just a few minutes ago."

"Thanks, guys." As I stepped inside, I made a mental list of the people I wanted to check in with. Charlie was at the top of that list and Marie Civiletti, my executive chef, was next.

I passed through the door that took me into the dishwashing station, a room equipped to handle a mountain of dishes quickly, efficiently, and in keeping with health department standards. Untold quantities of plates, silverware, glasses, cooking and serving utensils, and pots and pans passed through this room every shift. When I was younger, I often heard it said by people on TV shows and movies that if no other work came along, they could always wash dishes. Contrary to the notion that dishwashing was unskilled labor, running this operation required a lot of skill and was definitely not for the faint of heart.

I passed through another door into the main kitchen, which was a beehive of activity. What I first noticed was not a sight but a smell, specifically the heavenly aroma of baking bread. Our restaurant was famous for the bread baked daily and served as a complimentary part of every meal. Getting our old bakery chef back into the family had been among Charlie's most appreciated personnel moves. Working my way down the middle aisle, I saw three young people making salad—lots of salad! On the far aisle, our meat cutter was making quick work of a newly cooked roast beef that was still on the spit. As I reached the far end of the room and turned right, I saw Marie, who stood with her back to me. She was busy stirring something from a large pot on one stove. For a moment, I thought I had jumped into a time machine and gone back twenty-five years. Some things never change.

TWO DREAMS & OTHER TALES
Two Dreams

MARIE

Marie Civiletti came to Atlanta from Brooklyn, New York, in 1960, with her new husband, Dominic. Nine years later, she suddenly found herself a twenty-seven-year-old widow with five children to raise alone and no marketable skills except one: she was a remarkable cook. My dad had a good feeling about her and hired her for his kitchen. He learned what a find she was as she cooked various types of cuisine—though mostly Italian—which became quite popular with the patrons. Over the years, her leadership skills came to the fore, and she inevitably took over the kitchen. Though she had no formal training, Dad made her his sous chef—number two in the kitchen—and then executive chef when her predecessor retired. In the Civiletti home, everyone understood the kitchen was Marie's kitchen. At The Crossroads, we had the same understanding.

At fifty-seven, Marie was the eldest member of our working family, a distinction previously held by my father. In terms of years served, though, Charlie was still the senior member. Marie was a relatively short lady with a slightly heavy build and a wide, amiable smile. The hairnet she was wearing concealed a headful of hair that had once been long and black, but was now short and almost completely gray. While she could be tough when her kitchen duties called for it, she had a disarming personality that naturally attracted people to her. You couldn't know Marie well without loving her.

I liked to think that Marie was a typical Italian mother, but I couldn't tell you what a typical Italian mother was. I'm familiar with the stereotypes, but I know better than to go around spouting those. I can say that Marie was a devoted mother and grandmother and when she got excited, a steady stream of Italian would come rushing out of her mouth. Her eldest, Dominic Jr., was my best friend in high school. Through him, Marie was like a second mother. I sometimes called her Mama Marie—and still do—but was careful not to call her that in front of my own mother. Dominic learned to cook from Marie, and like her, made that his profession. Unlike her, he got a lot of professional training in the culinary arts, and being in high demand, moved around a lot. I had lost track of him some years earlier and only occasionally asked Marie about him. As a longtime mother, Marie had developed another ability I found almost scary.

TWO DREAMS & OTHER TALES
Two Dreams

She spoke without turning. "Are you going to just stand there staring at me, or do you have something to say?"

I laughed out loud. "How do you do that, Marie? Are you psychic, or do you have radar?"

She turned and gave me a wry look. "Noah, I've spent my life around children—lots of children. My little sisters and brothers, my kids, my grandkids, my nieces and nephews. If you're a mother with a lot of children around, you almost have to have a sixth sense to survive. Besides, I heard you coming and I know your footsteps."

"I'm impressed. The only reason I was staring was because seeing you there doing what you're doing brought back memories. When I was small, every time I came into this kitchen, you were standing right in that same spot stirring something in a pot. It was usually marinara, and it always smelled wonderful."

"I remember," she said with a smile. "You always had your tongue hanging out and looked like you hadn't eaten in years. Then your papa would come in and say, 'Don't even think of feeding that lunk-head. He gets plenty to eat at home.'"

I laughed again. "I always hated him for that. Not literally, of course. But, you know, the first time I had a birthday dinner here and got the full customer treatment, I discovered just how special an experience it was. I wouldn't have appreciated it as much if I'd been able to snack whenever I wanted to. Somehow, I think even then, Dad was preparing me to be the boss one day."

"Your papa was always a smart man, and a very generous one," she said. He helped me and mine get back up on our feet more than once." She stepped forward and put her hand on my shoulder. "I miss him, but I'm not losing any sleep, because I know you're going to take care of us all, just like he did."

Those words were so unexpected. "Do you really think so?" I asked.

She nodded. "Yes, I do. When I thought we'd lost this place for good, I cried for a week. I've been here thirty years, you know. When you

TWO DREAMS & OTHER TALES
Two Dreams

took over and made plans to open it again, you not only gave your papa his dream back, you gave something back to the whole family."

I hesitated, choking back my emotions. I wasn't so sure that what I had done so far justified her confidence in the future, but this wasn't the place to argue. "Then I guess I should start acting like the boss. How are things fixed up in here? Are you ready to go?"

"Believe me, we're ready. This crew here is green, but I'll have them whipped into shape in no time. Charlie told me we have reservations for 280 people tonight." A busy Friday or Saturday night usually brought in between 300 and 350. This was a Tuesday, so the word had obviously gotten out and folks were excited. She continued, "I put on a couple extra people to cover the overflow. Charlie thought you'd be OK with that."

"That sounds good to me. You don't know where Charlie is, do you?"

"He came through here a few minutes ago," she said. "He went out that way." She was pointing to the door that opened into the main dining room. I was beginning to feel like a hunter following a trail.

As I turned toward the door, Marie gently took hold of my right arm and looked me in the eye. "Noah, can I ask you something?" The change of tone had been abrupt and suggested to me we were about to have a serious talk. She asked, "How is Suzanne doing?"

I was immediately on my guard because I knew a motherly lecture was coming. "She's doing fine. I will tell her you asked."

She made it clear she would not be put off. "Are the two of you still living apart?"

"Yes, ma'am, we are. But it's a temporary situation."

She gave me a disapproving look. "Five months is a whole lot of temporary, Noah. That kind of thing can become permanent if you're not careful. Married people should be living together."

I took an exasperated breath. "It's not like that with us, Marie. We're not apart because we want to be. I'm opening a business here and she has

TWO DREAMS & OTHER TALES
Two Dreams

her work there. Now that The Crossroads is opening again, we're going to move back under the same roof. We just haven't figured out how we're going to work it out yet."

She shook her head back and forth. "My Dominic—God rest his soul—never spent a night away from me in nine years of marriage. If he'd moved away and left me behind, my papa would have hunted him down and broken his neck."

I said with tongue in cheek, "My father-in-law has wanted to do that to me since the day I stole his daughter from him." My attempt at humor failed, as Marie was not amused.

"Noah, I'm not trying to meddle here. I don't know your wife as well as I know you, but I love the two of you like you were my own. I'm unhappy about this because it makes you unhappy—don't think I haven't noticed—and I'm sure she doesn't like it much either."

"I hear you, Mama Marie. It means a lot to me that you care so much." She leaned in close and planted a motherly kiss on my cheek. I whispered, "You should be careful doing that in front of the help. They might think you're fooling around with the boss."

This time, Marie did laugh. She playfully slapped my arm. "Get out of my kitchen and go back to work." I grinned at her and she said, "Go on. Get going."

I turned and headed for the dining room in search of my floor manager.

RILEY

I met Suzanne Riley when we were both juniors at the University of Georgia. We were introduced by mutual friends. I was majoring in finance and she was pre-law. Of course, I'm biased now, but even then, I thought she was the most beautiful girl I had ever laid eyes on. She had long, auburn-colored hair, an ever-present smile, and the most seductive green eyes I've ever looked into. Once I got past the looks, I found her to have a sharp intellect, a quick wit, and a warm personality. I was hopelessly smitten, and

TWO DREAMS & OTHER TALES
Two Dreams

to this day, I still cannot believe she chose me from the long line of potential suitors who came her way.

Though we were both from Atlanta, we were definitely not from the same world. I was from a working-class neighborhood, while she came from a place much higher on the social register. Like me, she was her parents' only child. Her father, Harrison "Harry" Riley, was the senior partner at Branigan, Riley & Smith, an old Atlanta law firm co-founded by his father. She wanted to be independent from him, and yet was determined to be a big-time attorney just like him. Despite her background, she preferred to live a simple existence without the obvious trappings of wealth. Nowhere was this more obvious than in her appearance. When convention dictated she dress up, her fashion sense was exquisite and her affluence showed. When she dressed down, which was her natural state, she was a blue jeans, t-shirt, and often barefoot kind of girl, much to the dismay of her prim and proper mother. She liked things and people—like me—that were unpretentious.

At first, we politely and jokingly addressed one another as "Mr. Kemp" and "Miss Riley" (as in "Good day, Mr. Kemp" or "Nice to see you again, Miss Riley.") We eventually dropped the titles of address, but stuck with the surnames. The habit became so ingrained we still call each other Riley and Kemp to this day, much to the annoyance of my in-laws. They like the name Suzanne and insist I call their daughter by her *proper* name. Ironically, they both still called me Mr. Kemp long after I became a member of their family.

In the early years, my relationship with Riley was complicated. As undergrads, we engaged in a whirlwind romance while trying to get an education. After graduation, we went our separate ways for four years. I spent that time building a very successful career in Atlanta. Riley attended and graduated from law school and then established herself as a gifted litigator with a law firm in Charlotte, North Carolina. Her decision to settle that far from home wasn't popular with her parents, especially Harry, who hoped to see a third generation of Rileys in his firm.

Despite the distance, Riley and I never completely lost touch. In 1990, we finally got together again. After spending three months engaged

TWO DREAMS & OTHER TALES
Two Dreams

in a long-distance courtship, I moved to Charlotte and married her, which didn't make her parents happy. They had been hoping I'd moved on for good and that their daughter would marry a man of her own social standing. For eight years, we had a good life, but one persistent cloud hung over us: our attempts to start a family repeatedly failed. Despite our best efforts, Riley couldn't get pregnant, not even with help from doctors. As we reached our mid-thirties and saw forty on the horizon, we feared that parenthood would pass us by. We were considering adoption when the call came about my father, effectively putting our family planning on the back burner.

My desire to take up my father's mantel didn't turn out to be just a passing fancy. It became an obsession. The odd thing was that Riley was the one who urged me to go home to Atlanta and do what I needed to do for my dad. She assured me our marriage was solid enough to survive a little distance for a while. We agreed that once I got things set up in Atlanta, we would sit down and come up with a compromise plan that would solve the separation problem and work for both of us. With that, I headed home and got about the business of reopening The Crossroads.

During the five months I spent doing that, I was with Riley at least one weekend a month and spent countless hours on the phone with her. Marie was right, though; five months *is* a whole lot of temporary. Now that the business was opening again, it was time for us to have that talk. As much as I wanted to fulfill my father's dream, I wanted my wife back even more.

GERRY

As I stepped out of the kitchen, I found myself standing on the spot that commands the best view of the main dining room. The room lay along the south side of the kitchen and ran almost the length of the building. Directly across the room stood the main entrance, the maître d' station, the coatroom, and the waiting area. The door to the back hallway sat to the left at the far end. That hallway was where my office and the storage and utility areas were located. At the opposite end, the tall windows looked out onto Stratford Avenue. Stepping around the corner to the right, I could see through the entrance to the back dining room and down the length of that room as well. Though it was configured as two separate spaces, the dining area was, in fact, one large L-shaped room. What divided the dining areas

TWO DREAMS & OTHER TALES
Two Dreams

was a row of columns with a chest-high half-wall running between them. On the main dining side of the wall was a row of booths; on the back side, a large alcove we called the "beverage station." This was the place where nearly all the liquid refreshments we served were prepared, stored, and distributed from. The two notable exceptions were wine and beer. Those came from a side room whose door opened about halfway down the room along the right wall. With no more clues to Charlie's trail, that became my new destination.

The serving of alcohol at The Crossroads had been the subject of debate in the beginning. Being a good Baptist, Dad resisted experts who suggested that a successful restaurant needed a bar with a full-time bartender. He wasn't interested in running a tavern or turning his family restaurant into a watering hole. He conceded, however, that you couldn't have fine dining without a couple of draft beers on tap and a wine list. For this reason, his staff included a sommelier, or wine steward. In modern times, the role of the sommelier varies from place to place. At The Crossroads, he specializes in wine service, but also has responsibility for beer.

Since 1980, our sommelier had been a man named Gerald Phillips. Gerry started his career as a bartender, but soon found he cared little for that scene. He preferred wine to beer, so he spent the time, effort, and expense to get himself properly educated and certified as a master wine steward. After being apprenticed to the sommelier at a local country club, he came to The Crossroads. In nineteen years, he had become a fixture. He was very personable, and the staff liked him a lot. Many of the patrons regularly requested his advice on wine selection, and he was always happy to oblige. And, of course, he regularly consulted with Marie to come up with the wine list that went with the menu of the day.

I approached the room we affectionately called the "wine cellar." The name is a misnomer because it is not actually a wine cellar—or any other kind of cellar. This was the room in which Gerry practiced his craft. The double door into the room is wide and opens in halves at the top and the bottom. The bottom half has a shelf on it that can function as a bar top when it is closed and the top is open. I found the doorway fully open and

TWO DREAMS & OTHER TALES
Two Dreams

could see inside. There was a line of wine racks down the right wall. On the left, there was a door that opened into Gerry's office, a platform that had beer taps on it, with room for three kegs underneath, and a large refrigerator. On the far wall was a door that opened into an even larger storage area.

I called out, "Gerry, are you in here?"

I heard a faint voice call from the back room. "I'll be right out." Gerry had been working another job during the shutdown and had been back at The Crossroads for just a few days. We were both on the move all week and repeatedly missed one another, so I would be seeing him for the first time since Charlie brought him back.

He came out of the storage room and flashed a bright smile. Gerry was in his mid-forties, a tall man with graying hair and a neatly trimmed salt-and-pepper beard. Stepping toward me, he offered me his hand. "Hello. Good to see you, Mr. Kemp."

I tentatively shook his hand. "For twenty years, we've been Gerry and Noah. What's this 'Mr. Kemp' business?"

"You're the boss now. The boss was always Mr. K. You know that."

"Gerry, we are still friends and my name is still Noah."

"Maybe so, but in front of other employees, you're Mr. Kemp. You're the boss now, so get used to it." His smile got wider. "Now, what can I do for you?"

Since I had come as the boss, I couldn't argue about the name business, so I let it drop. I asked, "How are things going over here? Are you ready to go?"

Dad had told me that Gerry was usually very detailed when he gave his report. So, I wasn't surprised when he ran through his inventory, told me what he expected to serve the most of, and what he would need to replenish before the weekend rush. He also told me about some of the new offerings he had introduced because they had recently gained popularity. Though I know almost nothing about wine, he made the subject very interesting.

TWO DREAMS & OTHER TALES
Two Dreams

When he got done, I said, "Sounds to me like you're on top of it, Gerry. I think Dad was right when he told me you are the best at what you do. So, are you glad to be back?"

He looked at me for a moment, his eyes filled with emotion. He said, "I'll tell you, Mister... I'll tell you, Noah. I always loved this job, and I loved your dad. I hated parting with both, so words can't describe how grateful I am to you and Charlie for bringing me back. It won't be the same without Mr. K, but I think he's left us in excellent hands."

I thought for a second, then said, "You know, Marie nearly had me in tears a few minutes ago when she said the same thing. Do you really think I can make this work?"

Gerry nodded and said, "I do. I think we're all going to do just fine." When I gave no response to that, he changed the subject. "I've been meaning to call you because there's something I wanted to make you aware of. During the shutdown, I was working part time over at the country club, filling in for my old boss, who recently retired. One night a couple weeks back, I was serving a rather distinguished looking man. I didn't know him, but someone who knows me had apparently told him who I was. He asked me several questions about The Crossroads. You could have knocked him over with a feather when I told him you were back in Atlanta, reopening your dad's business. He made some nasty comment and quickly left. I got the impression he seriously dislikes you, but I couldn't for the life of me figure out why."

I grinned and said, "I only know one man who dislikes me that much." I reeled off a detailed description of my father-in-law.

"That sounds like him," Gerry said. "So that was the famous Harry Riley, huh? You two don't keep up with each other?"

"Understand, Gerry. Harry is a man of privilege. He's never forgiven me for turning his rich daughter into a commoner's wife, so we politely ignore each other—usually. He only knows about me what his daughter tells him and it would appear she didn't tell him about this. I knew somebody had because he called two weeks ago to gripe at me about leaving her."

TWO DREAMS & OTHER TALES
Two Dreams

Gerry suddenly had a worried look. "I hope I didn't cause you any problems," he said.

"Don't worry about it, Gerry," I said with a grin. "It's a small world, and he was bound to hear about it from somebody. Harry barks pretty loud, but he's harmless." Deciding to close out the conversation, I looked around and asked, "You haven't seen Charlie, have you?"

"Not in the last hour."

I thanked him, turned, and started back toward the main dining room. About halfway there, I changed my mind and parked myself at a table. I figured Charlie would happen by, eventually, so Mohammed could come to the mountain this time.

I sat and considered what had transpired since I returned from my errands. First, I had now gotten two votes of confidence from people I trusted. Still, I wasn't ready to jump on my own bandwagon. The other thing weighing on me was the obvious change in the way everyone addressed me. I was still Marie's little boy, but now I was also her benevolent master. To Gerry, I had gone from being his friend (Noah) to being his boss (Mr. Kemp). In the last five months, Charlie had deferred to me, something he'd never done before. I couldn't help wondering if I had earned all this newfound respect, or just purchased it with a lot of money.

CHARLIE

My reverie was interrupted by a familiar voice. "You look like a man with a lot on his mind." I looked up and there stood Charlie, the man I'd been seeking. "One of the biggest moments of your life is an hour away. Instead of looking eager and ready, you look troubled. Is there something I can do to help?"

"Do you have a minute to sit?" I asked.

"Just about a minute. Not much more." He took the seat opposite me. "What's on your mind, boss man?"

Not you, too, I thought. It was going to take a while to get used to being called "boss" by this man who had known me since birth. Rather than

TWO DREAMS & OTHER TALES
Two Dreams

dwell on that, I went straight to the issue at hand. "Are we all set to go tonight?"

"For sure. We are all supplied, the staff is all in place, Marie's got the kitchen buzzing. After five months of planning and work, we are as ready to go as we can be. Except that the boss doesn't seem to have his head in the game. So, I'll ask again, what's on your mind?"

I hesitated, trying to come up with the right words. I said, "When the two of us started down this road together in February, I was so eager. I couldn't wait for this night to come, but suddenly, it's like I've jumped off a cliff into a free fall. This was my father's big dream for a long time and he charged in with his eyes open. I arrived at the dream late and took little time to consider it before chasing it."

I waited for Charlie to say something, but he only sat and stared at me with that thoughtful look of his. I realized I would need to ask a specific question if I wanted some useful fatherly wisdom from him. I leaned forward and said, "Tell me something, Charlie. Do you think my father was wise to take a chance on me like this? I mean, I have no experience running a restaurant."

He sat back in his chair and crossed his arms, effecting a sort of half-grin. He was clearly amused by my question, though I wasn't sure why. He asked, "Did your old man give you this business or sell it to you?"

"He sold it to me. You know that."

He gave a slight nod. "How much do you still owe him?"

"I don't owe him anything. I got financing from the bank."

He leaned forward, narrowing the space between us. "So, let me get this straight. You walked away from a high-paying job and a promising career; put your marriage to that Riley girl on hold; talked some bank into giving you a sizable business loan; gave that money and a half-million of your own to your father to retire on; and you think *he's* the one who took a chance on you. I suspect those boneheads down at the bank might give you an argument."

TWO DREAMS & OTHER TALES
Two Dreams

I couldn't help laughing at that, and Charlie's grin only got wider. If anyone else spoke to me that way, I would take offense. But I knew him well enough to understand he was jesting. In good humor, I said, "I thought you were my friend."

The grin disappeared, and his expression became thoughtful again. "I *am* your friend. And your father is *my* friend; the best friend I ever had. Make no mistake, Noah. If he could retire without selling this place, there's nobody he'd rather bet on than you. He believes in you." He paused, then continued. "For what it's worth, I believe in you, too. So do all those folks who came back here to be part of the family again. But like my mama always said, 'all the confidence in the world don't mean much if none of it is your own.' Your father's all set and the rest of us can get work other places, but this is where you are going to make your mark, good or bad."

"Charlie, I still don't understand why you all have so much confidence in me," I said. "You, Dad, Marie and all the others. Like I said, I've never done this before. Why is everyone so sure I can be the next Mr. K?"

He thought for a moment before he spoke. "We have confidence in you because we know who you are, where you came from, who taught you to be the man you are, and what you've made of your life. You may not be trained for this job here, but you've been in business for a long time. You can do this. You just need to tell yourself that and believe it. Besides, there are a lot of veterans in this crew here ready to help you."

"What you said about making my mark. Any suggestions about how I go about doing that?"

He stood up and said, "Your father always seemed to have the right idea. Why don't you start there? Just start by doing what he did, and build on that."

I grinned. "You're a smart man, Charlie. You know that, don't you? Dad should have sold this place to *you*."

"Not *me*," he said, waving his hand, "I spent all I had putting two kids through college, the first ones in our family to go. I'm too busy saving for retirement now."

TWO DREAMS & OTHER TALES
Two Dreams

"You would've made a good boss."

"Maybe, but I've got my money on you."

Charlie gave me a reassuring pat on the shoulder and headed back to work. As he disappeared through the main dining room, I considered his words: *I've got my money on you*. Those words had more meaning than he realized. Charlie had been a member of The Crossroads family from the very beginning. My father hired him part-time as a sixteen-year-old high school student. Back then—in the mid-sixties—race relations in the South were at their lowest point. There were those who thought my father was asking for trouble by hiring a black teenager. Many of them didn't hesitate to say so, even in Charlie's presence. What they didn't know or didn't understand was that my father grew up in an inner-city neighborhood where *those* people were his neighbors. My dad was color blind regarding race, and besides, he'd known the Magruders his whole life. Except for two years in the Army during Vietnam, Charlie had been with us from the beginning, and this reopening meant everything to him. At fifty-one, he was too young to retire, but starting over with a new career or even a new job would be difficult. He had a vested interest in this business.

With all of that in mind, and the opening little more than an hour away, I stood up and headed for my office. In the main dining room, I encountered a crew of young folks—five women and three men—at work. They were setting all the tables and making sure that the room was in order. I stopped and chatted with them for a few moments. There were only three veterans in this crew; the rest were new-hires. Even in this place, a majority of waiters and waitresses were usually people in transition; that is trying to make a living while working toward something else, or studying for their *actual* career. Nevertheless, waiting tables can be a wonderful career—and profitable—for one with the discipline and people skills to do it well. Over the years, my father employed some of the best. As with everyone else I had spoken with that day, there was both enthusiasm and apprehension among this crew. New situations bring that out in people. I reassured them the best I could and thanked each of them for their service.

TWO DREAMS & OTHER TALES
Two Dreams

THOMAS

I made my way out the back door of the dining room and down the hall to my office. When I got there, I stopped in the doorway and took in the scene. Many times, I had stood on that spot and watched Dad working behind his desk. More often than not, he was busy with paperwork and required a knock to get his attention. Despite that, the door was always open, as he often told the staff. I stepped into the room and walked around behind the desk. I reached into the small closet on my left and came out with a solid maroon tie and a navy-blue vest emblazoned with The Crossroads logo on the right breast. My father always wore that combination with a white shirt when he worked the floor during the dinner hour. I put the tie on, making sure it was straight, and then the vest. Before I could button it up, the phone rang. I sat down in my chair and answered it.

An operator said, "I have a collect call from Mr. Thomas Kemp. Will you accept the charges?"

I grinned and said, "Yes, operator. I will."

A familiar voice came over the line. "Hey, son, how's it going?"

"Hello, Dad. How did you know I was thinking about you? And what are you doing calling me collect? Are you broke already?"

He laughed. "Oh, come on, now. You're the new business tycoon."

"But you're the one with the cash."

"I'll tell you what. Why don't I hang up and you can call me back?"

"Hilarious, Dad," I said, which started him chuckling.

"So, this is the big night," he said, turning serious.

"Yeah, this is it. We're opening at five." I paused, suddenly feeling very lonely. I tried not to let emotion creep into my voice. "I really wish you were going to be here tonight, Dad. It's just not the same without you."

"I appreciate that, son, but this is your night. You don't need me there confusing the issue."

"I wouldn't mind."

TWO DREAMS & OTHER TALES
Two Dreams

"I know that, Noah, but I would. You've worked hard for this. Besides, Joanne and I will be up this weekend. Would you book us a table for Saturday at seven?"

"Sure thing, Dad. I'll make sure they put out the best for you."

With reproof in his voice, he said, "You put out the best for all your customers, Noah. Remember, a satisfied customer—"

"—is a repeat customer," I said, finishing his sentence. "I haven't forgotten, Dad."

"Good, good. So, how's Charlie doing?"

"Well, he's wise, philosophical, and flip, as usual. But underneath that calm exterior, I can tell he's ecstatic to be back in the saddle."

"You take good care of him and he'll take good care of you."

"Will do, Dad. Will do."

"I haven't heard from Miss Riley in a while. How is she doing these days?"

I quietly shook my head. My father was the third person to bring her up in the last half hour—fourth, if you included my own mention of her to Gerry. I said, "Riley's doing fine, Dad. She plans to be here this weekend, so you'll get to visit with her."

"Good. I've always been partial to that girl. I guess I'd better let you get back to work. I just wanted to offer you our best wishes. We'll see you Saturday."

"Right, and give my love to Jo."

"Noah?" he said, the cheer suddenly gone from his voice. "Thanks for giving me back my dream. I always hoped you'd follow in my footsteps, but I'm sorry you had to buy the business from me to make it happen. It should have been your inheritance."

"Let's not start that again, Dad. No regrets, OK?"

"OK, son. Until Saturday. And good luck tonight."

TWO DREAMS & OTHER TALES
Two Dreams

I wanted to tell him I loved him, but the line clicked off. I hung the phone up and just stared at it for a moment. Despite what he said, I knew that letting go had been hard for my dad, and missing this night was harder still. His willingness to stand aside for the first time in thirty-five years and let me do it my way confirmed what Charlie had said about his confidence in me. However, I still wasn't completely convinced his confidence was well-placed. A part of me still wanted to turn back the hands of time and see my father in command, sitting behind this desk, shooting the breeze with the employees, and visiting with the patrons. But now, it was my turn to do those things.

RILEY & KEMP

I sat for a while, staring at a framed photo sitting on the desk. It was a picture of Riley, Dad, and myself taken on our wedding day. I couldn't forget how happy we'd all been on that occasion. This night's opening would be the second most important night of my life, and neither of them would be in attendance. The disappointment caused an ache that only deepened my anxiety. I understood why my father was staying away, but Riley's absence really hurt. Though I knew she would be arriving in three days, I had not seen her in three weeks and it seemed like forever. Besides, I really wanted to share this night with her.

I lowered my head into my hands and rested that way for a time until, suddenly, I heard someone quietly knocking. I looked up and couldn't believe my eyes. Like an answer to prayer, she was standing there in the doorway, smiling. Her presence was so unexpected that my hand flew up to my mouth and I let out a gasp. Her smile became a frown. "Do I look that bad?"

"Not at all," I said, my voice choked up. "You look perfect, as always."

Riley grinned. "The fashion police might disagree."

"That may be, but the fashion police don't love you the way I do."

She was dressed in a gray Georgia Bulldogs t-shirt, faded blue jeans with patched knees, and her favorite pair of thong sandals. She also had a gray suit bag draped over one arm and a shiny black pair of dress heels

TWO DREAMS & OTHER TALES
Two Dreams

dangling from the other hand. She hung the suit up on the coat rack and tossed the shoes into the corner. As she turned back to me, I came around the desk and met her halfway. We wrapped each other in a firm embrace that lasted a long time. She rubbed my back the way my mother always did when I was in this mood. I bit my lip and willed myself not to become visibly emotional.

As we drew apart and looked into each other's eyes, the look of concern on her face made me self-conscious. She said, "I spoke to Charlie out in the dining room and he told me he thought you were struggling. Mother has the cure, as always."

Without warning, she pulled me close and laid a long, hard, passionate kiss on me. It's kind of hard to explain the effect this has on me. After a moment during which I usually get light-headed, weak in the knees, and short of breath, the sun breaks through the fog and life becomes worth living again, no matter what my problems are. Then, I wonder for the millionth time what I did to deserve this angel.

It was no different this time. As we drew apart again, I said, "Same old magic. Thanks, darling." I quickly gathered my wits about me. "I wasn't expecting you today, but I sure am glad to see you. What brings you to my door?"

She looked into my eyes and gave me a gentle smile. "This is the most important night of your career, and you made me half-owner of this enterprise. To top it all off, I have some great news. So, I decided my other commitments could wait a couple of days. I'm here for you tonight, dear."

The part about great news got my attention, but I decided not to rush it. She'd get there when she was ready. Instead, I looked her up and down. "Something tells me you weren't in court today."

She laughed. "No, nor the office, either. By the way, everyone at the firm sends their best wishes for tonight. I actually spent most of the morning running errands and the afternoon making the mad dash down Interstate 85. I tell you I'm beat."

TWO DREAMS & OTHER TALES
Two Dreams

I took her hand, led her back around the desk, and gestured for her to sit in my executive chair. I pulled a straight chair from the back wall and sat facing her. She asked, "So, why are you in this mood today?"

"Stress. Fatigue. Anxiety. A big dose of fear."

She turned serious and asked, "What are you afraid of?"

I thought for a moment. There was a slight tremor in my voice when I spoke. "I don't want to make a fool of myself, or find out I'm not cut out for this, or disappoint my dad."

"You spent twelve years handling large amounts of other people's money," she said. "You even handled the portfolios of a few multimillion-dollar investors. I don't remember you ever having much in the way of jitters over any of that."

"None of those investors were my father."

"Here's some news for you, pal. None of the people currently invested in *this* business are your father, either. None of the people coming here for dinner tonight are your father. In fact, your dad would be the first to tell you it's all about the customers, not about him." Dad had said something of that nature not ten minutes before on the phone. She continued. "Kemp, if there are two things you know, it's business and people, and this venture involves both. When it comes to setting a good table and serving a first-rate dinner, Charlie, Marie, and the others know what they're doing. You have all the expertise you need here to make a go of this thing. With a little experience, you'll master it, just like your dad did."

I looked at her for a moment with my usual admiration. "How did you get to be so smart?"

She laughed. "I'm Harry Riley's little girl. You two may not care much for each other, but you must admit he's a really smart man."

I hesitated, then took a deep breath. "I've put off telling you about this, but I actually heard from Harry a couple of weeks back."

TWO DREAMS & OTHER TALES
Two Dreams

She was genuinely surprised. "Really? He's never called you before, has he? He always communicated with you through me. Besides, I didn't tell him you were back in Atlanta."

"Yes, I know. A little bird told him I was here reopening this place. I just learned today who that little bird was."

"So, what did Daddy say?"

"He rather pointedly asked my intentions concerning you. Was I leaving you or what? After I explained the situation to him, he implied that a woman's place is with her husband, and if I were a real man, I would fetch my wife home."

Riley's eyes widened, and she suddenly seemed very annoyed. "My father said that?"

"Not in those exact words, but that was the gist of it. Of course, I don't assume he's worried about our marriage. My guess is he sees this as an opportunity to coax his little girl back home, which is what he's always wanted."

She let out a heavy breath before she spoke again. "Well, he may get his wish this time, but it's going to be on *our* terms, not his."

I wasn't sure what she meant by that, but it seemed like a good opening. "Riley, since we're on the subject, I want to ask you something. When I came home and started all this, we agreed that once we reached this point, we would discuss our future and come up with a life plan that works for both of us. I've been alone long enough and I'm more than ready for that talk. What do you think?"

She held a long pause before speaking. "That's not really necessary. I've already made a plan and set it in motion."

That answer was completely unexpected. I didn't know whether to be relieved or hurt, happy or apprehensive. My only clue was her claim that she had great news. Finally, I asked, "What kind of plan did you make?"

"I submitted my resignation. July 31st will be my last day at the firm. This morning, I put the house on the market. I'm going to need you to sign papers for that, by the way. Once my business in Charlotte is done, I'm coming home to stay."

I was without words for a moment, unable to imagine what had brought this about. "Darling," I said haltingly, "I thought we were going to make this plan together. I wasn't expecting you to give up everything for me. What about your career?"

She was silent for a moment, then took my hand. "Kemp, do you remember when you asked me to marry you? I was amused because it sounded more like a merger plan than a marriage proposal. Part of your pitch was that you would come to Charlotte and live on my terms, so I wouldn't have to give up anything important to me. I asked you the same question about your career and you told me that you could do what you do anywhere there were people with money to invest, but you could only be with the woman you loved if you went where she went. When I said yes, you unplugged yourself from a very successful career here in Atlanta and reinvented yourself in Charlotte. You did all that so you could be with me and I could keep my dreams." For a moment, she seemed choked up. Finally, in a strained voice, she continued. "That's the most noble thing anybody ever did for me and I've never forgotten it."

She leaned forward. "It's your time now. You have a dream and I want to support you in it. As far as my career goes, I've had enough success that I can hang up my shingle pretty much anywhere I like. But I can only be with the man I love if I go where he goes. Well, you're here, so I've decided to come home. That's not giving up, it's compromise, and that's what people who love each other do. So, will you have me back or not?"

"Will I have *you* back? I thought I was the one who was AWOL." I shook my head and said, "Whichever way it is, I would be delighted for you to be my full-time roommate again. By all means, come home."

She squeezed my hand and smiled. "It's a deal, then."

"You know," I said, "you're pretty noble yourself."

"Don't be so quick to think so."

"Why not?"

TWO DREAMS & OTHER TALES
Two Dreams

She suddenly looked nervous again. "I still haven't told you everything yet. I don't want you to get me wrong, but this plan has been bouncing around in the old attic for a while now. There's a reason I kicked it into motion without consulting you first."

"And what is that reason?"

She picked up her purse, and after fishing around in it, came out with what I thought was a photograph. She handed it to me and said, "This was taken yesterday, but I've suspected it for nearly a week."

It took a few seconds for me to orient myself and see that it was, in fact, an image taken from a sonogram. Time seemed to stop for a moment. At last, I caught up. "Is this a baby?"

"That's not just any baby. That's going to be our first born. We're seven weeks pregnant."

It's hard to remember all of what happened during the next several minutes because it is still something of a blur in my memory. I had been emotional in a controlled sort of way since she arrived, but this news was too much. Between the anxiety of the day and the longstanding frustration of parenthood denied, I reacted in a way that even I wouldn't have expected of myself: I burst into tears. I hadn't done so since the day my mother died eleven years earlier. A lot of wives would roll their eyes and tell me to grow up and act like a man, but Riley had made this long journey with me and understood perfectly. She leaned in again, held on to me tightly, and sobbed with me.

When we finally calmed down enough to think rationally, we began a rapid-fire discussion of things that needed doing. First, the grandparents needed to be told. Riley assured me that relations between myself and her daddy were going to change for the better. Now that I was bringing her home and giving him his first grandchild, I was bound to become Harry's best buddy. No good deed ever goes unpunished, right? Then there was the matter of living arrangements. The two of us could hardly manage in my two-room apartment, much less raise a baby there. As soon as the house in Charlotte was sold, we were going to need a new one.

TWO DREAMS & OTHER TALES
Two Dreams

As for Riley's health, her doctor had told her that given her difficult history, he wanted her to spend as much of this pregnancy as she could off her feet. I seconded that notion and assured her she would get my full support. This brought us to finances. With Riley not working and most of my spare cash tied up in this restaurant, I was about to become our sole breadwinner and this business the source of that bread. It was time to get my head in the game, as Charlie put it, and believe in what I was doing.

Our discussion suddenly ran out of steam, so we just sat contentedly staring at one another. An irreverent thought struck me, and being unable to resist, I gave voice to it. "We spent eight years living together and couldn't make this happen. Now, we've spent five months mostly apart and here we are on the mommy train. You realize what this means, don't you?"

"No, what does it mean?"

"I should have left you years ago."

Riley doubled over and laughed so hard I thought she would hurt herself.

THE FAMILY

At 4:50, we walked into the main dining room together. Riley had ditched her casual clothes in favor of the suit and heels she'd brought with her. As usual, she looked perfect, without even a hair out of place. To borrow a commonly used phrase, my wife cleans up good.

I took in the assembled crowd and felt a wave of pride. Standing at the front were Charlie and Marie—the real bosses. I jumped right in. "Thank you all for joining me. This little gathering is what we call a muster, and it's an old tradition around here. It's the time when I tell you all how much faith I have in you—and I do—and challenge you all to do great things."

"Before I say anything else, I'd like to introduce someone." I gestured toward my wife. "Some of you know this lady, most of you don't. This is Suzanne Riley Kemp, my best friend, my better half, and my new business partner. She's followed me home to Atlanta to join The Crossroads family. I hope you don't mind working for a stockbroker *and* an attorney."

TWO DREAMS & OTHER TALES
Two Dreams

An unidentified voice called out, "God forbid." The room erupted in laughter. Even Riley thought that was funny.

"Many of you never met my dad," I said, "but you've undoubtedly heard the name Mr. K since you've been here. This place was my father's greatest dream, and he built it from the ground up with the help of some very dedicated people." I gestured toward Charlie and Marie, both of whom seemed a bit embarrassed by the attention. I continued. "His second greatest dream was that his son would one day take the helm. That almost didn't happen, but tonight that dream becomes reality, too. I appreciate you all helping me give him that.

"I've been in the business world for a long time, but I've never run a restaurant before. I don't have a formula for running this kind of business. But my dad did, and it worked for thirty-four plus years. So, that's what we're going with." For the next couple of minutes, I explained my dad's ideas for a workforce that served well and a clientele that was well-served. I asked them to join me in bringing a family atmosphere back to The Crossroads.

I reached into my vest pocket, came out with a key, and said, "When Mr. K got to the end of his muster speeches, which were never as long as this one has been"— everyone in the room chuckled —"he would pull out this key and quietly say, 'Everyone to your stations, please.' Then, he would go unlock the front door and welcome our first guests. That seems like a good custom to me, but on this one occasion, I'm going to depart from the script."

I gestured toward Charlie Magruder. "There's a man present who has been here longer than any of us. He helped my dad build this place up over the years and even picked him up and carried him from time to time. He's carried me a lot in the last few months, too." I stepped over to Charlie and held the key out to him. "Mr. M, would you do the honors tonight?"

There was a lot of emotion in Charlie's eyes as he stared at the key. Finally, he smiled and took it from me. "As you wish, Mr. K." He looked about the room for a few seconds, then said, "Everyone to your stations, please." He turned and headed for the front door, and the crowd dispersed in every direction.

TWO DREAMS & OTHER TALES
Two Dreams

Presently, I found myself alone with Riley and Marie, who hadn't left yet. Marie pointed at Riley and said to me, "So, I made that speech about her for nothing, didn't I?"

"Mama Marie, your wisdom is never wasted on me."

Marie turned to Riley and said, "You know, with your help, this boy is going to make his papa very proud. Tell me, dear, when are you due?"

Riley's eyes widened with surprise. "Late January."

Once again, I asked, "Marie, how do you do that? Are you psychic or something?"

She looked at me and rolled her eyes. "Noah, I told you about the children, didn't I? I've spent a lot of time around pregnant ladies and I know one when I see one. But don't worry. Until you tell your papa, nobody will hear it from me." She turned and gave Riley a motherly hug. "Congratulations, dear, and welcome home," she said.

"Thank you, Marie," Riley said, beaming.

After Marie left us, I looked around the room and said to my wife, "Charlie, Marie, Gerry, Dad, and you. All of you were right, you know."

"About what?"

"I *can* do this."

The Third Dream
Atlanta, 2014

It seems hard to believe I've been doing "this" for fifteen years now. Sometimes, it's hard to figure out where all the time has gone. Life has been so full and God has blessed us richly. The year after we took over The Crossroads, Riley and I became parents for the first time. Our first child was a son, and we named him Thomas Noah Kemp, after his father and grandfather. This pleased Dad greatly, but left my father-in-law with his nose a bit out of joint. The following year, we welcomed our second son and named him Harrison Riley Kemp—we even called him Harry, like his namesake. We tried for a third and hoped for a girl, but it wasn't to be. My

TWO DREAMS & OTHER TALES
Two Dreams

boys are now in their teens, and apart from my wife, they are my pride and joy.

Proving that God has a sense of humor, Tommy, who is named for two Kemps, is a typical Riley in many respects, including his desire to study and practice law like the three Rileys before him. Meanwhile, young Harry is the one who seems genuinely interested in the restaurant business. My dream—the third dream, if you will—is that one day my sons will be partners in much the same way my attorney-wife partnered with me to make The Crossroads a continuing success.

It was four years before Riley found her way back to the practice of law. Much to her father's delight, she joined his firm and quickly reestablished herself as a fine litigator, eventually making partner. Her father entered semi-retirement a few years ago. Though he doesn't really practice anymore, he has kept his office and passes through from time to time just to keep his hand in it, and to take his daughter to lunch whenever he can. Riley recently passed up a chance to sit on the bench, having decided she likes her life just as it is.

In July 2004, we celebrated the fortieth anniversary of The Crossroads in grand style. Unfortunately, Dad was not well enough to travel and be in attendance, and sadly, he died a month later at age sixty-eight. Though he wanted to see his grandchildren grow into adulthood, I suspect he still took pride in how life turned out for all of us. He saw his two greatest dreams come to pass, both successfully. Joanne brought him home to Atlanta for burial, but chose to continue living in Miami. I hear from her from time to time, and she seems to be doing well.

Marie Civiletti retired in 2010. She had been at The Crossroads for forty-one years and made dinner for untold numbers of people. We keenly felt her loss there in the kitchen, but felt she was getting a long-awaited and well-earned rest. Of course, Marie is not one to sit and rest for long. She spends most of her days chasing her grandchildren and great-grandchildren around. She doesn't cook as much as she used to, but it is impossible to keep her out of the kitchen entirely. One Sunday a month, she cooks for the whole Civiletti clan, which is quite an undertaking. On one occasion, when Riley and I were invited to join them, I noted with some surprise that the head of

TWO DREAMS & OTHER TALES
Two Dreams

the table in the crowded house was unoccupied. Forty years after his death, Dominic Sr. was still the man of the house and nobody sat in his place. I found myself incredibly touched that Marie maintained that level of devotion to her late husband so long after his passing. It made me appreciate my own spouse that much more.

We lost Charlie Magruder two years ago and still mourn his passing. He was a family man to the core and fiercely devoted to his own. He passed unexpectedly in his sleep one night—he was sixty-four years old. Except for his two-year hitch in the Army, he spent his whole adult life working at The Crossroads. One thing I've never forgotten is that nobody cried bigger tears than Charlie did at my father's memorial. Despite their widely varied backgrounds and the twelve-year difference in their ages, Charlie and my dad loved and respected one another liked no other best friends I've ever known. One interesting side note: I hired Charlie's son, David, to take over for him as floor manager, and he has proven to be a great catch. I've told Riley I wish I could get Dominic Civiletti to come home and take over his mother's old job. Then, we would have a family business in every sense of the word.

In the next few months, The Crossroads and Riley and I will all turn fifty. Naturally, we're planning another big blowout for the business. However, I doubt that our boys and the rest of the family will let our own milestones go unobserved amidst all the celebration. I'm sure there will be lots of cake, lots of cheer, and plenty of toasts to the two of us, as well as our business. Of course, I'll be saving the biggest toast of all for the man whose dreams made all this possible. Rest in peace, Dad. We'll never forget you.

TWO DREAMS & OTHER TALES
Two Dreams

Tale #3. Granddaddy & Me

An Overwhelming Loss
Michigan, May 2003

I sat looking out the window of the car as we passed the city limits. This wasn't just a leisurely car ride into the country for me. It was my passage into a scary and uncertain future. A couple hours earlier, I watched and listened as our pastor eulogized my parents, Johnny and Emily Truslow, and committed them to God and to the earth. It had been a week since a fire claimed the two of them and our house, leaving me orphaned and homeless at eleven-years-old.

My mother's parents, Mr. & Mrs. Garrett, sat in the front seats. Though they were family, they were strangers to me. I had met Grandma Betty briefly two or three times over the years, but had never so much as laid eyes on Grandpa Henry. I didn't know my Truslow grandparents or any of their family, who didn't even attend the funeral. As I understood it, the two families were like the Montagues and Capulets. Marrying against their parents' wishes made Johnny and Emily outcasts to both families. But, unlike Romeo and Juliet, they didn't express their love for one another by killing themselves. Instead, they raised their son—my name is Kevin, by the way—as devoted parents. I loved them dearly and the pain and fear I felt over losing them ran deep.

One matter requiring a quick resolution was finding a place for me. I no longer had a home or parents, no siblings, and no other close family. It seemed I would become a ward of the state and a citizen of the foster care system. But then Betty Garrett came on the scene and declared to the child welfare people that her only grandchild would not be raised by strangers. She was taking me home with her and that was all there was to it. The social workers had no issue with that and readily agreed. Now I was sitting in her car, being driven away from the only home I ever knew. However, I was not so young or naïve that I didn't catch on to one simple truth: my grandfather was not at all happy about the new arrangement.

TWO DREAMS & OTHER TALES
Granddaddy & Me

As the Detroit city skyline faded from sight, I felt a strange sense of doom. I was a city boy who had never been to the country before, much less lived there. The Garretts lived about two hours northwest of Detroit in a small rural town. My grandfather grew up there before moving to the big city as a young man and becoming a career firefighter. After retirement, he moved back to his hometown. His wife, Betty, was a Detroit native like me and had once undergone the same change of scenery.

***

I had fallen asleep and was jarred awake when the car door opened beside me. Standing there was my grandmother, her smile warm and welcoming. "Kevin, we're home," she said. I sat there frozen, unable to move. "You don't want to come out?" I still didn't respond, so after a minute, she closed the door again.

I could hear my grandparents' muffled voices outside the car, but could not make out what they were saying. Presently, the trunk opened and Grandpa Henry began unloading luggage. The door on the other side opened and Grandma Betty climbed in beside me, pulling the door shut behind her. She was silent for a minute, then looked at me with a mixture of sadness and concern on her face. She had just lost her daughter and now had a grief-stricken grandchild to deal with.

She put a hand on the back of my neck and stroked it. She leaned closer and said, "Kevin, I know this is hard for you. I won't say I understand your pain because I don't. I lost my mama and daddy like you did, but not at the same time and not when I was a child. I loved your mother and I've missed her so much, just as I'm sure you do now. But I love you, just as she did. You're safe here, and I promise I'm going to take care of you until you're old enough and ready to be on your own. Do you think we could start with that?"

A rush of emotion came over me and I lost control. I lowered my head, put my hands over my eyes, and wept loudly. My grandmother put her arm around me and kissed the side of my head. "My sweet little boy," she said through tears of her own. "You cry as long as you need to. We're going to get through this together."

TWO DREAMS & OTHER TALES
Granddaddy & Me

The Expedition
Michigan, November 2007

I was running late, and it was getting dark as I rushed down the sidewalk on Harper Street, headed for home. It was November, and Thanksgiving was one week away. The temperature had fallen, and the forecast suggested it might be a white Thanksgiving, which was not unheard of in our part of the country. My grandmother always encouraged me to think positively, but being thankful would not be easy this year.

Though I was in a hurry, I couldn't help stopping to take in a familiar sight. Across the street stood the wrought iron gate at the entryway to Oak Hill Cemetery. I had been uncomfortable around cemeteries since the day we buried my parents in one and hadn't been back to Detroit since then. Within these particular gates were two graves that were still relatively new. I was present for both burials, and with each, another member of my small family passed from my life.

The first occurred in June with the death of Ralph Garrett, my great uncle. Unlike his brother, Henry, Uncle Ralph lived in his hometown his whole life, as did his wife, Jane. In fact, they lived across the street from us. Ralph and Henry looked and talked a lot alike, and the two were very close. Uncle Ralph was a nice enough man, but he never warmed to me. I suspected that was because his brother never did. Besides brothers, the two men were hunting buddies, having been taught by their father as children. Every hunting season, they joined a third buddy and set off in search of white-tail deer. They always brought at least one home with them, so it was not uncommon for us to have venison for Christmas.

The second burial came just two months later. This one hit me particularly hard because the departed was my grandmother, Betty. Unlike Uncle Ralph, who suffered through a long illness, my grandmother had a massive stroke and promptly succumbed to it. I never forgot the day she sat with me in the back seat of the car and made her solemn promise to me. Though she didn't live to see that promise completed, she'd been as good as her word for the four years I lived with her. She had indeed made me feel safe and loved. She kept my life on an even keel, being almost as much of a mother to me as my own mother had been.

TWO DREAMS & OTHER TALES
Granddaddy & Me

After her death, I found myself in the sole custody of a grandfather who didn't seem to like having me around. The last four years had been a challenge because of it. In the early days, I attempted to ingratiate myself with him by simple acts of kindness, most of which were unappreciated. That usually drew my grandmother's ire and added to the tension level in our house. At first, I thought I was the cause of that tension, but something I overheard my grandmother say convinced me it had existed long before I arrived. My mother's long absence from their life had something to do with it, and my arrival had stirred the pot.

One way I helped keep the peace was by making myself scarce as much as I could. I immersed myself in a myriad of school and civic activities which kept me out until well after dinner most nights. I would come home and eat alone, then disappear into my room to do homework. Once Grandma Betty caught on to what I was doing and why, she started saving her dessert for later. She would join me at the table when I came in and talk to me about my day. Besides getting caught up, we'd use that time to plan activities the two of us could do together. Most nights, my grandfather sat in his chair in the living room watching sports, oblivious to what was going on in the kitchen. Given the close relationship I had developed with Grandma Betty, her death was the second greatest loss of my life.

***

The only thing I heard when I came into the house was the television playing in the living room. I peeked around the corner and saw my grandfather watching a taped replay of the Lions game from the previous Sunday. I checked the refrigerator and found our dinner. Aunt Jane had placed a casserole and tossed salad in there for us. On the counter was a note from her with instructions for preparing and serving them.

We had developed a new routine in recent months. Jane was at something of a loss after Ralph's death. She'd spent forty years taking care of him and their children in the way traditional housewives do. Caring and nurturing was what she did best. Suddenly, she had nobody to care for anymore and didn't know what to do with herself. When Grandma Betty died, Jane discovered new purpose as there were two single men next door in need of a motherly touch. More spontaneously than by plan, she took over the marketing for our household and began making and delivering dinner to us each day. I started coming home early each night, serving up whatever she prepared, and cleaning up afterward. My favorite nights were when she came over to prepare dinner, served it, and joined us for the meal. She was so much like Grandma Betty that I enjoyed having her around.

I heated the casserole, then my grandfather and I quietly ate dinner. Very little was ever said between us, not even at the table. It is surprising how fast dinner can pass when it is eaten in silence. He would finish his meal and then disappear into the living room, where he'd spend the rest of the evening. I would clean up and then do my homework. Since Grandma's death, he'd added a new element to this ritual. One night a week, usually Thursday, he took half a six-pack of beer into the living room with him and drank himself to sleep. Despite the longstanding contention between him and Grandma, he missed her desperately.

We were finished eating, and I was preparing to clear the table when my grandfather surprised me with a solicitous question. "I'm curious about something, son."

"Yes, sir?" I said. I usually called him *sir* because I'd always felt too intimidated to act familiar toward him.

"Before your grandmother passed, you rarely came home for dinner. You had so much else going on I could go for days without seeing you. Since her passing, you've been home for supper every night without fail, usually before dark. You've obviously put your regular life on hold and I was wondering why."

My gaze was fixed on the tabletop and I hesitated, trying to think of the right words. "I guess I just felt I was needed here, at least for a while."

"You think this old man can't prepare dinner for himself?" It wasn't said with anger or challenge, just curiosity.

"I don't know, sir. I've never seen you make dinner."

He chuckled. "You got me there. Still, I suppose it's lucky we have your Aunt Janie keeping us properly fed, huh?"

"Yes, sir."

TWO DREAMS & OTHER TALES
Granddaddy & Me

"So, what activities kept you so busy, anyway?"

I was still faltering a bit. "Well, sir. I've been in the Boy Scouts for three years."

"That's right. I've seen your uniform. It has an awful lot of badges on it. Your Uncle Ralph was an Eagle Scout, you know. Think you'll make Eagle?"

"That was my hope. I'm not so sure I'll make it now."

"What other activities did you have?"

"Science club," I said, finally feeling more at ease. "Drama club. School choir. I was also on the baseball team."

"Your grandmother told me you play catcher. Did she tell you I played the same position when I was a young man?"

"No sir. But, my mother did." I stopped and bit my lip, wondering if it was a good idea to talk about her.

He was silent for a minute before he spoke again. "I also played football, but I eventually got too old to play those types of sports. I suppose there are some who would call deer hunting a sport. That was always my passion. Your Uncle Ralph and me and our friend, Artie Davis, always spent hunting season together in the woods. But then, you already know that."

"Yes, sir."

"Unfortunately, Ralph is gone and Artie's not doing so well. With an old arthritic body and no more partners to lean on, I suppose my hunting days are over." He seemed to be talking mostly to himself now, no doubt mourning the losses he'd suffered over the last year.

After another moment of silence, he fixed his gaze on me again. "Your Aunt Jane tells me you have a birthday on Saturday. Which one is it?"

"I'm going to be sixteen, sir." I suspected he already knew that.

"Any plans for that day?"

"No, sir."

He stared at me for a long time, like he was working up to something. "Have you ever been hunting?"

"No, sir."

"Do you know anything about hunting?"

"No, sir."

"Would you like to learn?"

Unable to believe my ears, I said, "Yes, sir, I would."

He paused, then said, "OK. Why don't we go on Saturday? Would you like that?"

"Yes, sir, I would," I repeated, my enthusiasm overdone. I had no actual interest in hunting, but I was being offered the chance to bond with a grandfather I wanted so badly to be loved by. For that chance, I would let him teach me anything he wanted to.

"Do you have good boots and warm clothes? Plenty of layers?"

"Yes, sir."

"Obviously, you don't own a gun or have a hunting license, so you won't actually be hunting. You'll watch and listen and provide me with an extra pair of hands and an extra pair of eyes. I'll get in my last hunt and maybe you'll find you actually like it. How does that sound?"

"That sounds great, sir."

"Just one thing," he said with a touch of exasperation in his voice. "It's going to be an awfully long trip if you spend the whole day calling me *sir*. Would you have a problem calling me Henry?"

I thought about that for a few seconds. "My mother wouldn't approve of me calling you by your first name."

"She taught you to respect your elders, huh?" There was a bit of an edge in his voice, suggesting that something about my answer had struck a nerve. "Did she ever talk about me apart from telling you I played baseball?"

TWO DREAMS & OTHER TALES
Granddaddy & Me

"A few times."

"How did *she* refer to me?"

"She called you 'Granddaddy.'"

He was quiet a moment, then grinned and said, "Granddaddy, huh? I like that. Would you be willing to call me that?"

"Yes, sir. I mean, yes, Granddaddy."

"That's settled. You get yourself plenty of sleep tonight and tomorrow night. Five o'clock is going to come awfully early on Saturday morning. After dinner tomorrow, we're going to load up and I'm going to run you through the basics."

***

That night, I laid awake in bed, trying to make sense of what happened at dinner. I had begun the meal with a *grandfather* who didn't seem to like me and ended it with a *granddaddy* who wanted to take me hunting. Did all this mean we were friends now? If so, why now? Did Grandma's death somehow tweak his conscience over his neglected grandson? Or was he just lonely and desirous of company? Maybe he just needed a partner for one last trip to the woods. Maybe he decided that my turning sixteen obligated him to impart some fatherly wisdom, which would speed me on my journey to manhood. Somehow, I doubted that. Whatever the reason, benevolent, selfish, or otherwise, I had an opportunity I didn't want to miss. I was going to spend my sixteenth birthday getting to know my granddaddy.

***

Granddaddy was right. Five o'clock came early on Saturday. Despite getting a full eight hours of sleep, it was hard pulling my head off the pillow. As we ate a quick breakfast, and prepared bag lunches and coffee for the trip, I couldn't help wondering what Grandma Betty would have thought about all this. When we were finally ready, we climbed into Granddaddy's old truck and headed off to a place about thirty miles down the road. His old hunting ground was public land where a hunting permit was required.

TWO DREAMS & OTHER TALES
Granddaddy & Me

The night before, we had done as he said, loading up and running through the basics. We stuffed two backpacks with various tools, dry foodstuff, a couple of tarps, a length of rope and a blanket. A faithful Boy Scout, I packed a first-aid kit in mine. Granddaddy sharpened his hunting knife and even made sure his truck was in good running order.

He gave me the rundown on laws, rules, and customs that governed this type of activity, especially in a state forest. He told me about hunter's etiquette, clarifying that we might encounter others. We would need to respect their space and not interfere with their hunting. He explained to me the best way to layer my clothes to make it easier to shed them if it got warmer. He outfitted me with a bright orange vest, explaining that in the state of Michigan, hunters were required to wear orange to avoid shooting accidents. Those who wore camouflage, like my granddaddy, had to wear camo that was at least half orange. I naturally wondered—as any novice might—if this made hunters more visible to their prey. He told me that deer are color blind and wouldn't know the difference.

He also gave me a quick course on gun safety, even though I wouldn't handle a firearm on this trip. His weapon of choice was a rifle with a scope. I knew nothing about guns, so his description of the features and capabilities of his rifle were lost on me. I still listened carefully, though, when he told me the proper ways to handle it, loaded or unloaded. Hunter safety was too important not to acquaint oneself with these instructions and take them seriously.

As we finished loading the truck, Granddaddy pulled one other thing down from the wall. He told me this item was a deer sled, which he'd bought from a hunting supply store that day. He'd never used anything like it before, but in doing so, he was surrendering to old age. In their day, Henry, Ralph, or Artie would bring down a deer and Ralph would gut it. This would considerably reduce the weight. Then, they'd wash it out, take it by the antlers, and simply drag it home. With his partners gone and his own body slowing down, getting a fallen deer home presented a much greater challenge. Now, it was a matter of using a conveyance like this one to move the deer home and paying a professional butcher to dress it out. Times had certainly changed.

TWO DREAMS & OTHER TALES
Granddaddy & Me

The sun was coming up as we parked the truck in what was essentially a wide spot on the shoulder of a back road. We unloaded the truck and placed the backpacks on the sled, electing to drag them rather than shoulder them. We figured as long as we had the sled, we might as well make use of it and conserve our energy. I pulled the sled as we walked up a dimly lit, sloped path through the woods. I was following Granddaddy and observing him as we walked. He told me we had a little more than a mile to cover and I hoped he was up to it. After listening to him repeatedly mention his limitations, I wondered if he was exaggerating them or forcing himself to work through the aches and pains. He struggled, but didn't falter, so I suspected it was a little of each.

After a hundred yards or so on the path, we emerged into the open. It was full daylight by that time, though overcast. What I saw was a long meadow bordered on all sides by trees and covered with a thin layer of snow. Using the orienteering skills I learned as a Scout, I judged the meadow to be about a mile long and a quarter of a mile across. The right edge stood higher than the left. This, Granddaddy told me, was Taylor Ridge, a good place for hunting white-tail deer. The spot we were headed for was just inside the tree line, about three-quarters of a mile away.

As we slowly walked along the ridge, Granddaddy began pointing out various deer signs. There in the trees were the signs of a deer bed, a spot where a good-sized deer had just spent the night. He pointed out deer droppings, explaining to me that the very dark color showed they were fresh and that the color would fade. I noted strange markings on some trees, which, he explained, resulted from "rubbing." He told me that deer with antlers grow a layer of skin called velvet over them and that when the velvet begins to itch, the deer seeks relief by rubbing on the trees. Besides leaving scrape marks on the trees, it has the added effect of sharpening the points on the antlers.

It was after 7:00 a.m. when we reached our destination. There, just within the tree line, was a crude structure that served as a deer blind. Granddaddy explained that there were various methods of stalking and taking deer. One of them involved bellying up inside an enclosed structure that not only hid the hunter from sight, but concealed the hunter's scent from the very sensitive noses of deer and other wildlife. He and his partners had built this one a few years earlier. Since this was a state forest, they could not bring lumber in and build a permanent structure, so they used fallen timber to assemble this little roofless hut composed of four walls that stood approximately four feet high. There was an opening at the back and small windows carved into the other three walls.

Granddaddy told me that since this was public property, we had no claim to the blind. If we found another hunter there, we would have to keep moving. On that day, though, nobody was there. In fact, we had seen no one else at all that morning. As one might expect, the structure needed a bit of mending. After doing so, Granddaddy put one tarp on the floor for us to sit on and tied the other down over the top as a makeshift roof. With that accomplished, we tossed our packs in ahead of us and climbed inside.

***

We sat inside the deer blind for nearly three hours and took turns searching the scenery through binoculars. Granddaddy talked very little, choosing instead to concentrate on sights and sounds. When he talked, it was in whispers. We saw two does and a buck, all on the far side of the meadow, well out of range, and all of them traveling away from us. Finally, I spotted movement toward the closer end of the meadow, just outside the tree line. It was a buck with an impressive set of antlers.

"Granddaddy, look!" I said.

He took the binoculars and observed the deer for a moment. Finally, he said, "Wow! That is one fine buck—and a big one too. I think you found us a good one." He handed the binoculars back. "Take another good look at him." I did as he said. "If we take him, we're going to have to haul him all the way back to the truck. We don't shoot anything and then leave it behind. Do you think we can get him home?"

I had absolutely no idea, but I was game to try. I did my best to sound confident. "Yes, Granddaddy, I think we can." With that, I was committed.

"OK. He's still out of range, but he's coming this way. Let's watch him for a bit."

TWO DREAMS & OTHER TALES
Granddaddy & Me

A few minutes later, Granddaddy judged the buck to be in range. He pointed his rifle through the window and sighted on the deer. Before he could do anything else, he said, "Damn, he's changed direction. He's moving into the trees." He checked the view through the window behind him. "No good. Too many trees in the way. Are you up for a little hike in the woods?"

"Sure thing, Granddaddy."

"Then, let's go get him." He led the way out the back of the blind and I followed. Just as I stood up, I heard a distant noise that sounded like compressed air escaping from a tight space.

"What's that?" I asked.

"He's blowing," Granddaddy said. "That's a distress call that warns other deer that danger is close by."

"He knows we're here already?"

"I don't think so." His expression was one of cold calculation. "We might have competition, and maybe not the human kind." We heard the blowing again, though it was much louder this time. Granddaddy said, "He's on the move and he's coming this way. Come on."

As we rounded the front corner of our shelter, it happened without warning. I was standing about three steps behind him when I saw the buck over his shoulder, barely fifteen feet away and charging directly at us. I screamed, "Look out, Granddaddy!!" but it was already too late. The deer hit him head on, knocked him over, and trampled him. I attempted to dive out of the way, but it caught me with a glancing blow and tore a gash in my coat sleeve. I spun around and lost my balance. Not wanting to be trampled too, I jumped back up on my feet. By that time, the deer had covered a lot more ground and was disappearing into the trees.

I didn't have time to process what had just happened. I found myself immediately confronted with what had sent the deer into panicked flight. From the direction it had come, I saw a pack of grey wolves—five of them in all—coming at us, just like the deer had. Unlike the big beast, though, they were smaller and did not have the kind of momentum that prevented them from stopping. At the sight of two hunters in their path, one prone and one standing, they came to a halt, their prey instantly forgotten.

The five of them stood there, baring their teeth and growling. I'm not sure what possessed me to do it, but I ran forward and jumped over my granddaddy, placing myself between him and the wolves. The sudden movement caused all of them to jump back a step. I waved my hands in the air and yelled, "Go away!!"

This startled them, causing them to fall back again, though they continued to growl. I shouted a second time, but they gave no more ground. Without taking my eyes off of them, I dropped to a squat and began feeling around for my granddaddy's rifle. I found it, snatched it up, and slung it around, ignoring all of his instructions on proper handling. As I reached for it with my other hand, I accidentally brushed the trigger with my finger and the gun fired. I couldn't say which direction the bullet traveled, but the recoil caused the gun to jump from my hands. The sound was very loud, causing the wolves to turn and run the other way as fast as their legs would carry them.

I let out a heavy sigh, thinking I had just survived a close encounter with death—two of them, in fact. I would later learn that my fear of the wolves, though not unjustified, was overstated. Grey wolves avoid humans, especially hunters. They prefer to take down fleeing prey and often hesitate in the face of anything which stares them down. A man with a rifle in his hand is about the last thing a wolf wants to tangle with.

As I watched them go, I remembered my granddaddy. I turned and ran back to him. He was lying on his left side, his mouth and eyes both open and grimacing with pain. The first thing I noted was a three-inch gash on his forehead, which was leaking a lot of blood onto the ground. My scout training kicked in and I switched to autopilot mode. I ran to the blind and pulled out my pack, the contents of which I dumped onto the ground in front of him. I pulled the first-aid kit from the pile, pushed Granddaddy over onto his back, and hurriedly dressed the cut.

As I worked, I asked, "How badly are you hurt?"

He grimaced and spoke through gritted teeth. "Broken ribs."

TWO DREAMS & OTHER TALES
Granddaddy & Me

"Are you sure?"

"Yes, I've had them before. But this is worse because he also stepped on my bad knee. That hurts like the devil, too."

I finished taping down the gauze on his forehead and said, "I don't have a cell phone. Do you carry one?"

"Don't even own one."

"I can't call for help then. I'm going to have to move you myself."

"Listen to me, boy," he said. "That's too much for you. You could move faster if you left me here and went for help."

"That's a terrible idea," I said dismissively. "You're badly hurt and you could die out here if you're left unattended. Besides, I'm not leaving you for those wolves."

"Wolves are cowards. They won't come back."

"It doesn't matter if they're cowards," I said. "If you're lying here helpless, you'll be easy prey."

"I'm not *that* helpless. People don't die from broken ribs."

"Maybe not, but people *do* die from shock and exposure. I know how to deal with those."

He gave me a strange look, then grinned. "First aid merit badge, huh? Always prepared?"

"Something like that." I was indeed prepared, and unusually calm given the circumstances.

"And how do you plan to move me?" he asked sarcastically. "Carry me on your back?"

"Not exactly." I looked all around me, wondering if I could find enough materials to build a makeshift stretcher. Then, I remembered! I jumped up and ran behind the shelter, returning with the deer sled in hand. I held it up in front of him and said, "The Lord provides."

TWO DREAMS & OTHER TALES
Granddaddy & Me

Granddaddy rolled his eyes, but said nothing. I turned him back onto his side and pushed the sled up under him. He winced as I laid him back down on it.

For the next few minutes, I prepared for our coming journey. I pulled Granddaddy's pack out of the shelter and dumped its contents onto the pile I'd already made. I selected tools and things I thought I would need along the way and placed them in one pack. I put everything else in the other and tossed it back into the shelter. I would come back for it later if I could, or else some other hunter would claim it. I remembered my gun safety course from the night before. I made sure the rifle was cleared and unloaded before I put it on the sled beside its owner. I placed the blanket from Granddaddy's pack over him, tucking the edges up underneath him. I got my canteen out and gave him water. He didn't want any, but I made him take some anyway because hydration was important, especially if there was the potential of him going into shock. Finally, I put the pack on my back and prepared to leave.

I took hold of the rope and pulled the sled over the lip of the ridge. It moved down the slight decline, gaining momentum. Then, I turned us toward the far end of the meadow from which we had earlier come. The snow was a great help, but the load was still a heavy one and I was going to have to pace myself to keep from wearing out before we got where we were going. It occurred to me that, although I was now old enough to drive, I still didn't know how. Once I got Granddaddy to his truck, I'd have a whole new problem to deal with.

As I walked, my mind wandered and a lot of heavy thoughts came my way. This was my sixteenth birthday and I was pulling my injured grandfather to safety while trying not to lose him along the way. The chance I'd gotten to bond with him that day had felt like a real birthday gift and fate had stolen it from me, which seemed to be the story of my life. Even worse, this was my fifth birthday without my mom and dad, which made it even more difficult to endure. Since I was an only child, my folks shamelessly spoiled me and always made my birthday the most special day of the year. Though Grandma Betty remembered and celebrated with me each year, it wasn't the same.

TWO DREAMS & OTHER TALES
Granddaddy & Me

My mother, Emily Garrett Truslow, was just eighteen when she had me, barely out of childhood herself. Sometimes, she was like a big kid, always ready to roll around on the floor with me or play in the yard for hours at a time. Not that she wasn't a mature, responsible mother—she most definitely was. Though she could be very feminine when she wanted to be, she had a lot of tomboy in her. She was much more at home on a baseball diamond than at tea parties. She was much more herself wearing blue jeans and flannel shirts than dresses. She was tall and athletic, with short blond hair cropped at the bottom, bright green eyes, and an impish grin. Though I had many playmates my own age, my mom was my very best friend.

My dad, Johnny—nobody ever called him John—was the black sheep of his family. He had a hard-bitten, unpleasant father who was a Detroit fireman, just like Grandpa Henry. He also had two brothers and a sister. While his brothers were tough like their father, Johnny was the thoughtful and easygoing brother. While his brothers became firemen like their dad, Johnny did the unthinkable and became a cop; a Detroit patrol officer, to be exact. But marrying that Garrett girl was what got him tossed from the family. I never really understood why that was a problem for them and why it made us unfit to associate with. Whatever else he was, though, Johnny Truslow was my dad and my hero. The best part was that he desperately loved my mother and treated her like a princess. As long as the bond between the three of us remained strong, the world was a happy place for me.

Then came the fire. Ironically, it was the first time I ever spent a night away from home. I was invited to a sleepover with several other boys. The next morning, my parents and our house were gone. The next several days were painful and confusing. I was shuffled around from place to place while vain attempts were made to involve my father's family in the situation. One day, Grandma Betty showed up and took over, seeing that my parents got a proper burial and their little boy got a new home. It wasn't the happiest of homes, but as long as my grandma lived there, love was never in short supply.

***

TWO DREAMS & OTHER TALES
Granddaddy & Me

By my watch, we'd been moving for nearly twenty minutes and my guess was that we had covered about 300 yards. I did the math in my head and figured this would take us at least another two hours with rest breaks. This was assuming, of course, that I didn't give out first and that granddaddy didn't die on me. For reasons I couldn't understand, I had far more strength and stamina than I thought, like I was drawing on some kind of adrenaline reserve. Still, I needed a break, so I stopped. The trees we were moving toward were still more than a half-mile away, but to my tired mind, it seemed more like a hundred.

I pulled my canteen from my belt and took a pull from it. I dropped the pack from my back, took a few steps toward the sled, and looked down at my granddaddy. His eyes were closed, and he was deathly still. Though I had no reason to think he was dying, I had a moment's panic, anyway. Then he drew in a deep breath and opened his eyes.

"Oh, thank God," I said with relief in my voice. "You're still with me."

He cleared his throat. "Help me sit up, please." I sat him up and wedged my pack in behind him so he could lean against it. He rubbed his eyes and asked, "How are we doing?" I told him and he asked, "Do you really think you can pull me all the way home?"

I wanted to sound confident. "That's the plan. So far, we're keeping to it."

"Maybe so, but you're tired already, aren't you? I've already told you to go on ahead by yourself and send back help."

"And I've already told *you* that will not happen. You're the only family I have, and I will not lose you."

His eyes were fully focused now, and he fixed an impatient stare on me. "You just don't get it, do you, boy?! It's my fault that we're both in this mess!"

"Granddaddy, what happened with the deer was an accident. It's nobody's fault."

TWO DREAMS & OTHER TALES
Granddaddy & Me

"Listen, son!" he said, his voice getting louder. "This whole trip was a fool's errand. I'm not fit for this anymore and I have no business being out here. But I just had to do it one more time, so I brought you along to be my crutch. You've never been hunting in your life and now, because of my stupidity, you're at risk, too. If anything happens to you today, I'll have one hell of a lot of explaining to do if I ever see your mother or grandmother again. What you need to do is put your pack back on and go home. If you see a ranger, send him my way. Then, go home and live your life. If I don't make it back, it won't be the worst thing that ever happened to you."

Though his words made him sound benevolent and self-sacrificing, I wasn't convinced. For four years, I'd dragged around a question I didn't dare ask anyone, not even Grandma Betty. Two days earlier, I'd put that question aside, believing I didn't need it answered anymore. Now it was back. I asked him, "Why do you hate me so much?"

He looked at me like I had slapped him. "Why would you think that?"

"Until two days ago, you never gave me any reason to think anything else. And now, it sounds like you just want to be rid of me. What would you think if you were me?"

He shook his head and said firmly, "I don't hate you. I've never hated you."

"Then I must have offended you somehow."

He shook his head again and whispered, almost to himself, "It was never about you. Not directly."

"Then who was it about? It was about my mother, wasn't it? It was all about her, wasn't it?"

He looked at me wearily. "Why do you think that?"

"When I was a little boy, I asked my mom why we never visited you. She told me she broke her daddy's heart; broke it so bad that he wouldn't forgive her. She didn't tell me how. I was awfully young, after all. When I moved in with you and Grandma, the first thing I noticed was that nobody wanted to talk about my mother; not in front of me, anyway. I thought she was a forbidden subject, but I didn't know why. What did she do, Granddaddy?"

"Please don't ask," he said, closing his eyes. "It's too hard to talk about."

Suddenly, I felt anger rising inside me. I threw my canteen down, dropped to my knees, and leaned forward until I was directly in his face. I clenched my teeth. "Granddaddy, you want to talk about what's too hard? Let me tell you what I think is too hard. For me, it was hard being a sensitive child who couldn't understand why his family wouldn't love him. Little kids always blame themselves for that sort of thing. For me, it was hard seeing my house burned to the ground; knowing my parents died in there; wishing I'd gone to heaven with them rather than being left behind by myself. For me, hard was living for four and a half years in the house of a grandfather who couldn't stand the sight of me; always feeling like I had to walk on eggshells around you; always afraid of saying the wrong thing to you; always feeling like the safest thing to do was to hide in the shadows where you couldn't see me. For me, hard is having you finally offer me your hand, only to have you pull it back and tell me to go away."

I sat up straight. "Granddaddy, I've spent my whole life being punished for my mother's sins without knowing what they were. I've paid the price and I have a right to know. What did she do to cause all this misery?"

He stared at me for a moment before he finally spoke. "It wasn't your mother. Not really. It was mostly me. It was what I did to her; what I did to all of us." He closed his eyes again and took a deep breath. "Betty and I wanted to have children so badly. We thought we would make great parents. It wasn't easy, though. We struggled for ten years and lived through many disappointments, including two miscarriages. We had just about given up when God finally blessed us with a child. I became a father at thirty-three." His eyes opened again, and he looked at me. "I wanted a boy, but we got a girl. I tried to act disappointed, but the first time I held Emily in my arms, I fell in love. She was my little miracle and you couldn't have paid me enough to give her back. The joke was on Betty, as she wanted a girl, but Emily became *daddy's* little girl. After she started walking, she followed me everywhere, like a faithful puppy.

"I didn't know what to teach a girl, so I taught her what I knew about; mostly about baseball, football, and other sports. Once or twice a year, I'd take her to Tiger Stadium to see the Tigers play, and she loved it. I taught her to build and fix things. I took her to the firehouse many times. I told her that even though we didn't have any women firefighters, there was no reason she couldn't grow up to be one if she worked hard. Once when she was twelve, I brought her here with me from the city and took her hunting with us. What a mistake that was. After watching me shoot a deer and her Uncle Ralph gut it, she never ate venison again.

"One thing I didn't teach her about was boys—and that was my biggest mistake. She never disobeyed me until she took up with that Truslow boy over my objection."

"What did you have against my father?" I asked.

He stared at the ground briefly before he spoke. "It wasn't him specifically. It was that family of his. I came up through the ranks in the fire department with Joe Truslow, your other grandfather. Joe never should have been a firefighter because he didn't have the right mindset for it. He was vain and full of himself, had a violent temper, and had the foulest mouth you ever heard. He thought the whole system was rigged against him. Whenever someone got rewarded and he didn't, he wasn't happy for them and would undermine them to anyone who'd listen, so nobody liked the man. For reasons I never understood, he took a particular disliking to me and even got his wife into the act. Betty stopped coming to family events because Joe's wife was always so catty and ugly to her."

"My dad wasn't like the rest of them," I insisted.

Granddaddy looked at me silently for a moment, then said, "Emily met him at one of those events and they were immediately taken with each other. My pride got the better of me and all I could think was that I didn't want any of those damned Truslow boys around my little girl. I assumed they were all like their father. I repeatedly warned her off, but she defied me. Then, the unthinkable happened."

TWO DREAMS & OTHER TALES
Granddaddy & Me

"She got pregnant, didn't she?"

"You knew about that?"

"I was born just three months after they got married. It wasn't hard to figure out."

With a sudden rush of anger, he said, "She was eighteen years old, unmarried, and getting pregnant. Why did she do that? I tried to counsel her on what to do next, but she was determined to marry that boy. I got my blood up and told her she would do so over my dead body. Well, she went and married him anyway and I told her never to come back. She asked me to understand about the marriage and to please forgive her for the rest. I turned to stone and wouldn't listen. She finally stopped coming around and we didn't hear from her anymore."

He took a deep breath. "Betty never forgave me for driving Emily away. It poisoned our marriage. She was a religious woman and would never think of leaving me, but life in our house was never happy again. When I retired ten years ago, I thought if we moved out here, we could start over, but nothing changed. I finally decided I wanted my little girl back, and that it was time to beg her to forgive me for what I did. But my foolish pride held me back long enough that I didn't get to it in time. She probably died hating me. When Betty set out to bring you home with us, I allowed it because I felt I owed her and Emily that much. You think I couldn't stand the sight of you? That's not what it was at all. You look so much like her. I cringe every time you look at me. I don't hate you. I hate myself. I never meant to hurt you, son, and I'm so sorry I did."

I looked at the ground for a moment, then said, "My mother didn't hate you, either. She wanted you back, too. When she told me about breaking your heart, she said she wanted to make things right, but she didn't know how. That was the only time I ever saw her cry. Granddaddy, at the end, you both wanted the same thing and all you had to do was reach out and take it."

"Well, I can't fix it now, can I?"

TWO DREAMS & OTHER TALES
Granddaddy & Me

"You don't have to fix it! The two of them are in a better place and they're not worrying about us anymore. It's just you and me now. What are we going to do about us?"

He looked away from me and mumbled, "I just don't know, son."

I leaned closer and said, "Let's get one thing straight. My name is not *son*, and it's not *boy*. I'm your grandson and my name is Kevin. Do you have a problem with calling me by my name?"

He didn't respond. He was pale and clearly still in pain. I could tell all that talk had taken a lot out of him. It was time to finish this and let him rest while I got back to my task.

I stood up and said, "Our old lives end today. Like it or not, I'm going to haul you all the way home. When you're well enough, you're going to decide. We're going to be a real family or no family at all. I won't stay where I'm not wanted. Now, if you don't mind, I have work to do."

I helped him lay back again, then put my canteen on my belt and my pack on my back. At the front of the sled, I took hold of the rope and pulled again. I knew immediately I had two problems. The rest break had taken too long and my muscles were all tightened up. It would take a couple of minutes for the blood to flow again and for me to regain momentum with the sled. The other problem was that those same trees in the distance now looked like they were a *thousand* miles away.

***

I was pacing outside the examining room my granddaddy had been taken into nearly an hour earlier. I was growing impatient and could hardly contain myself. I suddenly heard a familiar voice calling my name from a distance. I turned to see Aunt Jane rushing down the corridor toward me. Even before she reached me, I felt a stir of emotion and the tears started. She wrapped me in a tight embrace and held me that way for a moment. Finally, she pulled back and looked into my eyes. She placed her hand on my cheek and said, "My poor boy. Are you all right?"

"Yes, ma'am," I answered. "I'm just tired."

TWO DREAMS & OTHER TALES
Granddaddy & Me

"I'm sure you are. Don't worry. I'm going to take care of everything now. How is Henry doing?"

"I don't know. He has broken ribs and a busted-up knee. He's in there, but nobody has told me anything yet. I'm getting really worried."

"These things take time," she said. "If I know Henry, he's giving them a run for their money in there."

"It's funny you should say that. I didn't realize how stubborn he was until today."

She grinned. "Come on over here." With her arm still around me, she led me to a small couch that sat against the far wall and we both sat down. She said, "You told me on the phone he had a run-in with a deer? What exactly happened out there?"

Thankful for the distraction, I told her a carefully edited version of the story, leaving out the parts about confronting wolves, Granddaddy urging me to leave him behind, and the argument that ensued. I hadn't finished the story yet when the door to the examining room opened and a tall doctor in a white lab coat came out. I jumped to my feet and sprinted over to him. His nameplate identified him as Charles Walters, MD, FACS.

"You must be Mr. Garrett's grandson," he said. "Rather than lying quietly like I told him to, he spent much of the last hour telling me all about you. His examination was a challenge."

I offered him my hand, and he shook it. "I'm Kevin Truslow," I said. I turned and gestured to Aunt Jane. "This is Mrs. Garrett, my aunt."

He looked at her, confused. "You're his wife?"

"No," she said, "I'm his sister-in-law, his late brother's wife."

"Oh, I see. Well, I'm pleased to meet you both. I'm Dr. Walters and I've been examining him."

"How is he doing?" I asked.

"He has three broken ribs on the right side. We'll need to set those and wrap him up good and tight. Fortunately, they didn't puncture the lung. The bigger problem, though, is that knee. We got x-rays, and it looks like a torn cartilage, but we'll need to get an orthopedist to have a good look. Whether he needs repair or replacement of that joint, he'll be staying with us for a while."

"He'll need rehab after that, won't he?" Jane asked.

"Yes, he will, and all the support you can give him." He turned his attention to me. "I'm curious about something. Either your grandfather is delirious—though I don't think so—or the two of you have had a very unusual day. Did you really stare down a pack of wolves and run them off?"

Aunt Jane gasped and put her hand to her mouth.

"Granddaddy's rifle did most of the talking," I said.

"He also told me you dragged him on a sled for nearly a mile."

"It wasn't quite that far. Near the end, a ranger came along and took over. He called in others and they helped me get Granddaddy here."

"You're a very modest young man, but make no mistake. Though neither of these injuries were life-threatening by themselves, you still saved your grandfather's life today."

As though on cue, the door opened, and a gurney rolled out with my granddaddy lying on top of it. As it passed us, the doctor held up his hand, and it stopped moving. He looked at my aunt and me and nodded.

Granddaddy was pale and tired-looking, but awake. The gash on his forehead was now held shut with paper tape. He was taking shallow breaths, no doubt because of the pain. He weakly held out his hand to me and I took hold of it. Quietly, he said, "You're a good boy. Don't let anyone tell you different. Not even me."

"I won't, Granddaddy."

"I was very proud of you today. You're a good man to have in an emergency; especially when it involves a stubborn old fool like me." He paused. "Kevin, I regret never saying it before, but I really do love you." He paused again. "Hell of a birthday, huh? I'm sorry I didn't get you a real birthday present rather than treating you to this little disaster."

Granddaddy & Me

With a tear in my eye, I said, "You just gave me the only present I wanted, Granddaddy. I love you, too." I leaned down and planted a kiss on his cheek.

He said, "About that decision you asked me for today. When I come home, we're going to be a real family—you, me, and your Aunt Janie. I think Betty, Ralph, and Emily would want it that way."

"And Johnny, too?"

"Yes, Johnny too." He looked up at my aunt. "Janie, would you look after my boy for me?"

She smiled and said, "You've got it, Henry."

We watched as they wheeled him down the corridor. At the end of the hall, they turned the corner and passed from sight.

A Patchwork Family
Michigan, December 2015

It was two days before Christmas, and it snowed for most of the day. Though I had never liked snow that much, it certainly seemed appropriate for the occasion. As I pulled into the driveway and parked, the old house looked the same as always except for the blanket of white on the roof, the bushes, and the front yard. The walkway was buried too, which meant we would have to traipse our way to the side door. At some point, I would need to come out with a shovel, carve out a path, and unload the trunk. In spite of all that, I was happy to be home.

It had been an eventful month for me. I completed all of my classes, my thesis, and my oral exams. In a solemn ceremony, I received my master's degree from the University of Michigan, bringing my post-graduate education to an end. I also received a lucrative offer of employment from a firm in my hometown of Detroit. I would soon be returning to my roots.

The most important thing I gained that month, however, was seated next to me. I turned and smiled at my companion, who smiled back. Her name was Angela Hartley, and we'd become inseparable over the last year. During the previous week, she had also become my fiancé.

TWO DREAMS & OTHER TALES
Granddaddy & Me

"Are you ready for this?" she asked.

"Absolutely."

"Will they be happy?"

"Absolutely."

"Do you think they'll be surprised?"

"Absolutely not. I've been bragging about you for more than a year. I think they'd be surprised and disappointed if you weren't wearing that ring by now. What do you say? Shall we go join the folks?"

We entered the house through the side door and found ourselves in the mudroom. We stomped the snow off our feet and removed our coats. As we stepped into the kitchen, I called out loudly, "Is anybody home?"

Nana Jane appeared from the living room, a wide, excited smile on her face. "Kevin, darling," she practically shouted. "Welcome home." She approached and embraced me. "It's so good to see you." She continued the love fest, placing a big wet kiss on my right cheek.

"You remember Angela, don't you?" I asked.

"Of course, of course." She embraced her as well. "Welcome, my dear. I'm so glad you could join us for Christmas."

Angela said, "Thank you for having me, Mrs. Garrett."

Nana took hold of her hand and examined the diamond ring on her finger. Her face broke out in a wide smile. "You know, Kevin's grandmother wore this ring for forty-four years."

"Yes, he told me," Angela said.`

"What did I tell you?" I said. "Not the least bit surprised."

Nana Jane quickly changed the subject. "Your granddaddy is napping in the living room, but he should come around shortly. It's a cold day out there. Can I get you both some coffee?"

"That sounds perfect," I said.

TWO DREAMS & OTHER TALES
Granddaddy & Me

We sat down at the kitchen table for a bit, drinking coffee, talking about school, and sharing our preliminary wedding plans. We'd barely gotten started on those.

It had been six years since Aunt Jane went from being my surrogate grandmother to being the real thing. She and Granddaddy got married right before I went off to college, though it wasn't a conventional marriage. They weren't romantically linked the way each had been with their lifelong spouses, but they were very fond of one another. The decision to marry was prompted by my imminent departure and their mutual need for companionship and support in their old age. They both understood that when their time came, each would be laid to rest in the place already prepared for them. I was relieved because I didn't want Granddaddy living alone with all of his physical challenges. To everyone's delight and surprise, their domestic partnership eventually blossomed into a real marriage.

The hard part for me was figuring out what to call Aunt Jane after the wedding. It was awkward to call my grandfather's wife *Aunt* Jane. It was even more awkward to call her "Grandma" since she was living in my real grandma's house. It was Jane herself who suggested I call her "Nana," like her other grandchildren did. I tried it on for size and took to it right away.

We'd been chatting over coffee for a while, when Granddaddy called from the living room. "Janie, is that Kevin out there with you?"

"Yes, Henry," she called back. "He and Angela just got here a short while ago."

"Well, what are you waiting for? Send them in here."

Nana laughed and said, "The master calls. You know the way."

I took Angela's hand and led her into the living room. Granddaddy was rising from his easy chair, his cane resting in easy reach. Following his run-in with the deer on Taylor Ridge eight years earlier, he'd had surgery on the knee and rehab, but never regained full use. Over time, the knee became very arthritic, and he got around the house on a cane with great difficulty. For excursions, I'd gotten him a wheelchair. At first, he'd been too proud to be seen that way in public, but once he finally tried it, he

TWO DREAMS & OTHER TALES
Granddaddy & Me

discovered he enjoyed being squired around. He still longed to have his mobility back, though.

He smiled widely. "Come over here, my boy."

Granddaddy may not have been steady on his feet, but he could still give bear hugs with the best of them. By the time he let me go, I was practically gasping for breath. He said, "I see you brought Miss Angela with you. Come over here, young lady." She stepped over to him and he planted a polite peck on her cheek. Without warning, he asked her, "So, has my grandson popped the question yet?"

I was completely taken aback. I said, "Granddaddy, that's awfully forward of you, don't you think?"

"I'm an old man. I don't have time to wait while you beat around the bushes. So, what's the verdict?"

I looked at Angela and said, "Go ahead. Show him."

She smiled brightly and held out her hand for him to see. I saw great emotion in his eyes as he stared at Grandma Betty's ring. He said, "You know, darling, the day I gave Kevin that ring, I told him that I hoped I would live long enough to see it rest on the finger of a deserving young lady. I guess I can cross that one off my list now."

He sat back down, while Angela and I sat on the couch facing him. I said, "Don't forget that there's one more thing on that list, Granddaddy." He looked at me, confused. "You gave me that ring the day you married Nana Jane. I was your best man, and I agreed to do that job on one condition."

"Oh, Kevin, you're not going to hold me to that, are you?"

"I certainly am. I was your best man and now you're going to be mine."

"Kevin, I can't even stand on my own two feet most of the time."

"Granddaddy," I said, "you don't have to be able to stand on your feet to be the best man in the room. You only need a pocket big enough to

TWO DREAMS & OTHER TALES
Granddaddy & Me

hold the ring and a mouth big enough to say a toast everyone in the room can hear. You can do that, can't you?"

"I suppose. Where is this event going to take place?"

"The wedding will be at Angela's family's church in Ann Arbor. The reception will take place at their house."

Granddaddy thought for a moment. "Kevin, you know I don't travel well anymore. Ann Arbor is a long way."

"You're coming to our wedding," I said. "If I have to, I'll get out that old deer sled and drag you all the way there."

He laughed. "You're just stubborn enough to do that, aren't you? You're like your mother—and your granddaddy."

TWO DREAMS & OTHER TALES
Granddaddy & Me

Tale #4. Three Days at Sunset

Arlington National Cemetery
Virginia, July 2008

It was a warm, humid, and overcast day as we made our way down Eisenhower Drive. It was my mother and me walking hand-in-hand behind the caisson that was bearing my brother to his final resting place. Mom was dressed in black and I was wearing the dark blue full-dress uniform of a US Navy lieutenant commander. As an enlisted Marine, Randy wouldn't normally have been accorded full military honors, but he died in combat, making them appropriate. Besides the horse-drawn caisson, the procession included an escort platoon and a military band, which played as we walked, announcing the passage of a fallen hero.

At one point, we passed a tall silver pole topped by a round, black marker which announced our arrival at Section 59. On our previous trips to Arlington, this section had always been our destination. This time, though, we were going a little further. My gaze swept across the sea of white gravestones in that section, one of which bore the name of my father, Gunnery Sergeant James Dillard, USMC. Dad deployed with 1st Battalion, 8th Marines to Beirut in 1983. The 1/8 was part of a multinational force of Americans and French sent to serve as a buffer between warring factions. Certain local Muslim militias chose to view the presence of the peacekeepers as an occupation, and so the shooting began. On October 23, a suicide bomber crashed a truck laden with explosives into the Marine compound, destroying the barracks and killing more than 300 people, including 241 Americans, mostly Marines. Dad narrowly escaped that disaster, but fell just a few days later to a sniper near Beirut International Airport. On a late fall day that year, we had come to this place to bury him.

Now, we were doing it all again. Randy had deployed to Afghanistan three times in the six-plus years since September 11, 2001. On a hot, dusty road outside of Kandihar, his convoy was struck by one of those roadside bombs the Taliban used with devastating effect. While some of his mates survived with debilitating injuries, Randy never knew what happened to

TWO DREAMS & OTHER TALES
Three Days at Sunset

him. I realized the parallels between him and Dad were quite eerie. Both served in the Marines, rose to the rank of sergeant, fought in the Middle East, and died at the hands of men who claimed loyalty to Allah. Finally, both were killed without warning by people they never laid eyes on.

At first, I was angry, declaring that only a coward would kill with a remote-controlled bomb. I was then reminded that, as a US naval officer, I was part of a military machine that had an arsenal that could deal out death from tens, hundreds, and even thousands of miles away. Nowadays, we could fight whole wars without ever seeing the eyes of our enemy. We may have been more sophisticated and efficient at it than the Taliban, but that didn't make our brand of war making any less brutal, just more civilized. As General Sherman once said, all war is hell.

Randy and I were four years apart in age, but were very close. Me being a sailor and him a Marine made for a persistent, yet friendly rivalry. When we got together, words like 'squid' and 'jarhead' regularly passed between us, but always in jest and with great affection. It made no difference that I was an officer, and he wasn't, since we never crossed paths in any military setting. At family gatherings, the only rank either of us answered to was "brother"—as in big brother and little brother. Though I outranked him, I respected and deeply admired my brother for the job he did. In a shooting war, it was men like Randy whose boots hit the ground and carried them into the thick of it. Though as his brother, I also held my breath and worried a lot, just as our mother did.

We came at last to Section 60, the piece of ground reserved for men and women lost in what President Bush called "the global war on terror." These were the casualties from Operations Iraqi Freedom and Enduring Freedom, and other related conflicts. The flow of arrivals from Iraq and Afghanistan had been continuous for six years. As important as many believed it was, the war on terror was waged at fearful cost. So many had been lost and our military resources were stretched out thinner than they had been since Vietnam.

After we took our places at the burial site, the casket team slowly and methodically removed the casket from the carriage and brought it forward. All present stood and saluted. There were only two of us in the

TWO DREAMS & OTHER TALES
Three Days at Sunset

family seats. Dad had been gone for twenty-five years and Mom never remarried. My wife, Linda, who loved Randy like he was her own kid brother, was back home in San Diego, recovering from major surgery. Our son and daughter, both still in high school, were caring for her. As for Randy's family, there wasn't any to speak of. He was once married to a nice lady named Sherri, but she stopped being nice when she realized she could no longer deal with his long absences. During his second tour of Afghanistan, she moved out and took everything with her. After the divorce, Randy never heard from her again and never quite got over it. With nothing to keep him at home, he volunteered for a third tour, a decision which ultimately cost him his life. That day, it was just Mom and me watching over my little brother, like old times.

The flag was raised from the casket and the officer-in-charge invited us all to sit. A military chaplain stepped forward and spoke. "Dearly beloved and honored guests," he said, "we have come to this place today to lay to rest our brother, Staff Sergeant Randall James Dillard, and to commend his soul unto God. Christ once said, 'Greater love hath no man than this, that a man lay down his life for his friends.' Sergeant Dillard laid down his life not only for his friends and his comrades, but for all of his countrymen."

What followed was a short, but very effective sermon about the mercy of God and the assurance of a blessed life beyond death. As children, Randy and I regularly worshipped, took communion, and said confession at St. Mary's Parish Church in our hometown near Cleveland. I was even an altar boy for a time. Despite all that participation, neither of us grew up to be overtly religious as adults, which often put us at odds with our mother and my wife. On the day of my brother's burial, though, I found myself comforted by the chaplain's words. I know my very devout mother took solace in them as well.

The officer-in-charge asked us all to rise for the presentation of military honors. I stood with my mother and raised my hand to my brow in a standard military salute. A short distance off, a team of seven men armed with rifles extended those arms and fired a volley, followed by a second and a third. It was a twenty-one-gun salute, the ultimate show of respect for a fallen infantryman. As each volley was fired, my mother trembled. Talk of guns and the sound of gunfire had been difficult for her to endure since losing her husband to a sniper in Lebanon. For me, it had a strange effect as well. For a brief instant, I was carried back to another time and place with a different set of gunners making themselves heard.

Ohio, July 1984
TUESDAY

The shots from the rifle range were coming almost continuously. It was amazing how much noise a dozen preadolescent boys could make when you put rifles in their hands. Given that they were city kids with little or no shooting experience, I doubted the paper targets they were firing at were in any real peril. I had elected to sit outside and wait until our boys finished up and came out because I wanted no part of that activity.

It was our third day at Camp Sunset. We had come in on Sunday afternoon and set up for six days of cabin living, water sports, outdoor activities like swimming, hiking, shooting, and archery, and various demonstrations performed by invited speakers. It was a chance for a bunch of city youths to experience the great outdoors and breathe a little clean air. Our group hailed from the urban town of Miller Heights, one of the many commuter enclaves that make up the suburbs of Cleveland.

Camp Sunset and its sister, Camp Sunrise, sat on the northern shore of Swanson Lake, which was about a fifty-minute drive from downtown Cleveland. The two-camp complex was owned by the state of Ohio and had once served as a weekend training facility for the state National Guard. No longer used by the Guard for that purpose, the state was now making the facilities available for use as summer camps by local municipalities. Under that arrangement, our own City Youth Authority moved from the Youth Center in Miller Heights to these two camps for one week each July, hosting up to 120 local kids. Sunset was the boys' camp and Sunrise was for the girls. Between them was a stand of thick woods about fifty yards across, with a single path cut through it. These woods were informally known as "No Man's Land." This was a reference to the regulation that each gender was to remain on their own side of the zone, unless conducting official business.

TWO DREAMS & OTHER TALES
Three Days at Sunset

The children attending camp from our town ranged in age from six to fifteen. They took part in programs designed for two separate age groups: six-to-ten; and eleven-to-fifteen. I was fifteen years old that summer and few kids my age were still coming to camp. I shared my cabin and my days with eleven younger boys, ages eleven to thirteen, and a seventeen-year-old staff counselor. I hadn't wanted to come, but I did so as a favor to my recently widowed mother. I was there mainly to be my brother's keeper and everyone in camp knew it.

Randy, eleven that year, had always required careful handling. As a small boy, he was the sensitive child who cried when he got left behind, didn't get picked for a sports team, or didn't win at games that required someone to be the loser. He cried harder when people picked on him, no matter how innocently. By eleven, he had mostly grown out of it, but not fully. He hadn't learned to handle extreme adversity well, so he'd go into his shell when he was being physically or verbally assaulted. If you pushed him hard enough, you could still get a few tears out of him. That was why bullies had so much fun with him. Unfortunately, the world had no shortage of those, not even at Camp Sunset. Randy's nemesis that week was a thirteen-year-old named Jimmy Warren.

As an active-duty Marine, my father wasn't around a lot. When he was, he tried to teach us how to be strong, proud, and self-reliant young men. Randy's unwillingness or inability to take such teaching to heart exasperated Dad. Whenever Randy complained about those who picked on him, Dad would inevitably tell him to stand up for himself, but that kind of discussion never ended well. My mother saw it differently, telling Dad not to worry so much about Randy; that he would grow up when he was ready to. I fell somewhere in the middle, wanting to see Randy take a stand, but never hesitating to get between him and anyone bullying him. He was still my little brother after all, and I never let such people forget it. I couldn't always be there to protect him, though.

The single most traumatic event in our family life was Dad's sudden death in Beirut. Publicly, at least, Mom showed the bravery and strength one would expect of a Marine wife. I had the difficulties one might anticipate for a teenage boy who had tragically lost a father he was close to.

TWO DREAMS & OTHER TALES
Three Days at Sunset

It was Randy who was most affected, though. Despite their different personalities, he worshipped Dad and wanted his approval more than anything. Dad's death put him in an emotional tailspin, which he was only just pulling out of.

Mom's attitude concerning Randy had changed noticeably. She decided that what he needed was to spend more time around boys his own age, and hopefully, around some new male role models. She worked mighty hard to talk Randy into going to camp and even had to promise him that his big brother would come along. I learned about that promise after it was made, but I still agreed to it. And so, that Sunday afternoon, she took us to the Youth Center, kissed us goodbye, and put us on the bus to camp. Knowing my mother, she went home and cried all week. It couldn't have been easy for her to push her "sweet little one" out of the nest.

A deep voice broke in on my thoughts. "Hello, Luke. How's it going today?"

I looked up and saw before me the face of Herman Morris. He wore a lot of different hats back in Miller Heights, but everywhere he went, they called him Coach. As director of boys' summer programs at the City Youth Authority, he was camp director when our boys came to Camp Sunset. During the academic year, he was a popular social studies teacher at the high school, as well as head coach of the varsity football team. He was a solidly built African-American who, despite being middle height, was a very imposing figure. Whether on the football field, in his classroom, or at camp, there was never any question who was in command.

A former Army Ranger, Coach Morris left the service after a tour in Vietnam, having been permanently disabled by an enemy bullet. Surgeries on his right knee and a lot of physical therapy made it possible for him to get around, though with a slight limp. As a teacher and coach, he was both tough as nails and as compassionate as they come, a rare combination. He could reach down inside the toughest football player or student and get just a little more out of them. And yet, he could also counsel troubled kids effectively with a soft touch. Despite the scowl he sometimes wore, he was quite affable.

"Hello, Coach," I said. "I'm doing all right, I guess."

TWO DREAMS & OTHER TALES
Three Days at Sunset

"You didn't want to shoot targets with the others?" he asked.

I hesitated, then shook my head. "No. I'm afraid that when I look down the barrel of a rifle, the target will look like my dad. I bet that sounds crazy to you."

"No, actually it doesn't. Life is full of unexpected reminders of things we'd rather not think about. Trust me, I know. So, how are you and your family coping these days?"

I took a deep breath. "It's been hard for Randy. For the first couple of months after Dad died, he cried an awful lot. We were already sort of used to that, but this was different. He calmed down after a while, but he is still pretty depressed most of the time. Mom thought sending him here for a week would help, so I agreed to bring him."

"And how is she coping?"

"Not as well as she wants us to think," I said. "She used to cry a lot too, mostly at night when she thought we were asleep. She smiles when we're around her, but I know she still hurts a lot. I wish I could do more to help her."

He patted my shoulder. "Don't sell yourself short. Your being there helps. I'm sure you do plenty for her. And you can bet she's sleeping a lot easier knowing you're looking after your brother this week."

"Do you think so?"

"I do." He looked at his watch and said, "I'm afraid I have some place else to be. Listen, if you need to talk, come see me. Here, at the Youth Center, at school, wherever. I'm a busy man, but I can always make time."

"Thanks, Coach."

He turned and strode off toward the waterfront. No sooner had he disappeared from sight than another familiar face appeared. It was Kyle Weston, the staff counselor assigned to the boys in our cabin. Kyle was seventeen and in his second year working with boys at the Youth Center and here at camp. I knew him from high school, where he was seen as cool by those who liked him and as a jerk by those who didn't. At the Youth

TWO DREAMS & OTHER TALES
Three Days at Sunset

Center, when he wasn't working, he liked to pump iron to keep himself looking muscular. He was one of those guys who spent a lot of time admiring himself in front of the mirror. In the summer, he was often without a shirt, his physique on display. Even those who liked him agreed that Kyle Weston was full of himself. At school and around town, there was usually at least one girl with adoring eyes hanging on him.

"Was that the coach?" he asked.

"You know it was, Kyle," I mumbled, rolling my eyes. I knew what was coming next.

"What did he want?"

"Nothing. We were just talking."

"Oh, yeah? What about?"

One thing I didn't like about Kyle was his habit of giving me the third degree about things that didn't concern him. I was convinced it was driven by paranoia, the fear that we were all talking about him.

I said, "We were talking about how my family is doing since my dad died. Would you like to hear what I told him?"

He ignored my sarcasm. "We have free swim after this until 9:00. I may need to run some errands. Can you keep watch until I get back?"

This question reminded me of the thing I most disliked about Kyle: he was lazy. Apart from pumping iron to impress people, he had absolutely no ambition or motivation. He considered counseling older boys to be the perfect job because to him it was like babysitting boys who were old enough to supervise themselves—and he got paid for it too. Of course, that kind of thinking didn't work with that age group unless chaos was the goal. That attitude had gotten Kyle into trouble with Coach before and kept him perpetually on probation. And yet, Kyle never learned his lesson. For this camp season, he had the extra benefit of having a camper—me, that was—who was almost old enough to be a counselor himself, making it possible for him to dump his responsibilities and disappear whenever he felt like it. He had been doing so every day since we arrived. Eventually, Coach would catch on and bounce him for good. Hopefully, our boys wouldn't end up as collateral damage.

Before I could answer Kyle's question, my brother emerged from the rifle range.

"Luke! Luke!" he shouted. "Look what I did." Randy ran across the open space to us, waving a large piece of white paper. He was dressed in khaki-colored shorts, a dark green t-shirt, and blue sneakers with white stripes. His wavy blonde hair was ruffled, and he was very excited. He handed me the paper to look at.

"See this?" he said. "I hit the bull's eye!"

It was a target sheet with a neat hole almost perfectly centered on the target. A second hole was in the outer ring. A snowbird could be seen on the bottom right corner of the page. God only knew what the other seven shots hit. Though it was clearly a one-in-a-million lucky shot, Randy was very proud of his accomplishment.

I smiled. "Looks like you killed it, buddy. Good job."

His smile got wider. "I can't wait to show Mama. Do you think she'll be proud, Luke?"

"You can bet on it, little brother. Make sure you put that in a safe place so it won't get messed up." Randy ran off and joined the other boys.

I was pretty sure proud wasn't the right word for what Mom would feel. The sight of bullet holes on a paper target would not be a welcome sight to her. Still, Martha Dillard had been a mother for a long time and was a pro at it. Her little boy would get the smile, hug, and praise he wanted from her. Whatever pain that caused her, she would put aside and deal with when she was alone. One day, Randy would be old enough to understand the subtleties of the situation.

It seemed Mom had been right about camp being a good experience for him. His engagement with the other boys and his excitement over the target shooting were a welcome departure from his demeanor of recent months—and years. I saw very little of the lethargic child who usually slouched when he walked, and who stared at the ground and mumbled when

TWO DREAMS & OTHER TALES
Three Days at Sunset

people tried to talk to him. Still, we had an ongoing problem that was sure to hinder that progress.

I looked at Kyle and said, "Since we have a moment, can we talk about Randy's problem with Jimmy Warren?"

Kyle rolled his eyes. "Oh, no. Not again. What is it with you and that boy, anyway? I know he's a tough little kid, but he's not a bad kid and not the troublemaker you say he is."

"What rock are you living under, Kyle?" I asked. "Jimmy is a nasty bully who picks on kids that are smaller and weaker than him. He even has a partner, Eddie Baylor. This week, they've made my brother their favorite target. I'm getting tired of telling them to leave Randy alone. The only reason they keep at it is because they know I can't touch them and you won't do anything about it."

He shook his head. "I don't see it that way, Dillard. They're normal kids. Sometimes they argue, make faces at each other, and even fight. But until they throw real punches, I'm going to let these boys be boys and not worry about it."

"You know what I think, Kyle?" I asked as I stood up. "I think if it did come to real punches, you still wouldn't worry about it. You know why? Because you don't know what you're doing. I wonder why Coach can't see that. Maybe I should talk to *him* about it."

I didn't wait for Kyle to react. I turned and walked over to our group of boys as the last of them came out of the rifle range. Presently, Kyle joined us and we formed up two lines to head back to our cabin. We didn't get very far before the trouble started. There was a tussle at the front of the line and a pair of hands shoved Randy, causing him to land in the ditch on his hands and knees. His target page had fallen from his hand and lay on the gravel road. I was not surprised when Jimmy Warren stepped out of the line to taunt him.

"Boy, Randy. You're real clumsy," he said. "You should watch where you're going." He looked down at the paper on the ground. "Hey what's this?" He stomped his foot down on it and began mashing it back and forth, causing the gravel stones to shred it. "What a shame."

TWO DREAMS & OTHER TALES
Three Days at Sunset

I ran up to them and stopped a few feet away. "Warren, keep moving!" I said.

He looked at me and then at Kyle. It was clear Kyle wasn't going to say anything, so he grinned at me, then turned and ran off to rejoin the other boys. I bit back a curse, then lifted my brother to his feet. "Are you OK, Randy?"

He didn't answer. Instead, he was fighting back tears and losing the fight. A thorough check convinced me that he had no scrapes or cuts. I lifted the paper from the ground and gave it to him. He angrily balled it up and threw it into the ditch. He then stomped off in the direction the other boys had gone.

I picked up the ball of paper, straightened it out the best I could, then carefully folded it and put it in my pocket. Kyle was standing a short distance away watching me. We just stared at one another for a few seconds. Then I shook my head in disgust and walked away.

***

Our boys got into their swim gear and headed for the waterfront. No sooner had we settled in than Kyle headed off on his "errands." I noted that his route took him toward the boathouse, but I couldn't imagine what business he had there. When he passed the place without stopping, I was confused. The only thing further along that shore was the infamous No Man's Land. Beyond that was Camp Sunrise. Surely Kyle wasn't dumb enough to risk getting caught over there—or was he? I turned my attention back to the boys. Though there was a lifeguard on duty, the counselor was required to keep his eyes peeled when his boys were in the water. It wasn't my job, but someone had to do it in Kyle's absence. Camper safety was too important to neglect.

For the two hours we were there, Randy sat with me on the sand because he had never learned to swim. I'd hoped he would learn that week, but he wouldn't go into the water, especially with the other boys around. At 9:00 p.m., the lifeguard blew his whistle and declared the beach closed. We gathered up our stuff and headed back to our cabin. When we got to the admin building, I sent the boys on ahead and went inside. Kyle hadn't

TWO DREAMS & OTHER TALES
Three Days at Sunset

returned, so I was picking up our group's Order of the Day for Wednesday. I got back to our cabin just a few minutes later.

When I stepped in the door, I could see Jimmy Warren was at it again. This time, he'd been joined by his flunky, Eddie Baylor, who was standing by his bunk, holding a sneaker in his hand. Rushing toward him was my brother, shouting, "Give me back my shoe!" Just as he reached Eddie, the sneaker flew into the air just out of his reach and into the hands of Jimmy. It was a classic game of keep-away, an exercise intended to torment its victim while providing great amusement to the tormentors. I had never understood the thinking of people, especially children, who enjoyed hurting others.

Before I had the chance to tell him to knock it off, Jimmy let fly with words that changed the whole situation. Waving the sneaker toward Randy, he said, "You know, you're real dumb, Randy; just like that dumb jarhead father of yours. What kind of idiot stands in the open when people are shooting at him? No wonder he's dead."

For a few brief seconds, it was deadly quiet in the room. Suddenly, I heard myself screaming. "Warren, you little creep!!" Everyone turned toward me and I saw in their eyes a collective look of fear. Randy burst into tears and ran for the door. As he passed me, I reached out and tried to take hold of his arm. He brushed me aside and charged out into the night, wearing nothing but his swim trunks. I decided to let him go for the moment. I turned back to Jimmy and gave him my most menacing stare. Then I advanced toward him, slowly, but purposefully. He got wide-eyed and began backpedaling, literally backing himself into the corner. When I got close enough, he held out the sneaker, as though it were a peace offering. I snatched it from his hand and threw it across the room.

I bared my teeth. "I don't know why you want to hurt my brother so bad, but you just stepped way over the line. How would you feel if I said nasty things about *your* father in front of all these boys?"

His look of fear changed to defiance. "I don't care. I hate the bastard!"

TWO DREAMS & OTHER TALES
Three Days at Sunset

That was unexpected, and for a few seconds, I was at a loss for words. I thought I would shut him up, but had only pushed one of his buttons instead. Remembering what had made me angry, I said, "I'm sorry to hear that, Jimmy, but Randy and I loved our dad, and we are proud of him because he fought and died for this country. They awarded him medals and buried him at Arlington and—" I paused, wondering why I was bragging to this little bully. I bunched up my fists and put the menacing stare back on. "From now on, my father is off-limits! You will never disrespect him again. Understood?!"

Jimmy nodded, the fear having returned. I walked over and reached into Randy's foot locker, digging out a clean t-shirt and a pair of socks. I then retrieved both of his sneakers and headed out the door to find him. He'd only gone as far as the backyard. It was a fairly large clearing, bordered by a low-lying stone wall that separated it from the thickly wooded hill behind it. Randy was sitting at the far end of the wall, crying. I walked over and put the clothes down beside him. I touched his shoulder and whispered his name. He leaped to his feet and threw his arms around me. He continued to cry unabated for a while. Affected by his distress, I wanted to cry myself, but I kept my composure.

Finally, he sniffled. "He shouldn't have said that about Daddy. He had no right."

Technically, he did have a right, but that didn't make saying it appropriate. I said, "Randy, he won't say anything else about Dad. I put the fear of God in him."

The tears started again. "I miss Daddy," he said. "It hurts so bad sometimes."

"I know, buddy. I know what you mean." We stood there for a while before he finally drew back from me. I pointed at the clothes and said, "Randy, put these on, please."

"I don't want them."

"Randy, the mosquitoes are terrible out here. They'll eat you alive, so please put them on."

TWO DREAMS & OTHER TALES
Three Days at Sunset

Rather than argue the point with me, he sat down and pulled the t-shirt on while I got down on my knees and put the socks and sneakers on his feet. Once all of that was done, Randy sniffled again and asked, "Luke, can we go home? I want to go home."

I'd half-expected him to ask that. "Randy, it's after 9:30 and nobody's going back to the city tonight. And Mom doesn't even know where this place is. Can you hold on until morning? If you still feel this way, we'll go talk to Coach Morris tomorrow and maybe call Mom and talk to her." He nodded agreement.

I stood up and said, "I'll tell you what, Randy. I'm beat. I can hardly keep my eyes open. You want to come in with me now?"

"No, I want to stay out for a while."

My guess was that he wasn't ready to face the other boys yet, so I didn't press him. "Well, don't stay out too late, OK? And please don't wander off and get yourself lost."

I turned and headed back into the cabin.

WEDNESDAY

I woke up just after 6:00 a.m. on Wednesday morning, almost an hour before reveille. I rolled over and looked at Randy's bunk. When I drifted off to sleep the night before, most of the boys were still up, and neither Randy nor Kyle had come in yet. My brother was now lying face down and fully dressed on top of his bedcovers.

"Are you awake, Dillard?"

Startled by the unexpected voice, I rolled over the other way to see that it was Kyle, sitting on the edge of his own bunk. He was wearing nothing but a dark blue pair of boxer shorts. He had something in his hand, but in the dim light, I couldn't make out what it was. "Just barely," I said. "What do you want, Kyle?"

He stood. "I need to talk to you before the others wake up. Come on outside with me." Without waiting for a response, he walked to the cabin door and stepped out into the daylight.

TWO DREAMS & OTHER TALES
Three Days at Sunset

"Sure, Kyle," I muttered. "Thanks for asking." I climbed out from under the covers, pulled on a t-shirt and sneakers, then got up and walked to the door. As I stepped outside, I could see the sun was up and the sky was clear. There was a slight nip in the air, but that would change within an hour. Kyle was sitting on the stone wall, his muscular chest—and most of the rest of him—on full display. He was puffing on a cigarette, seemingly oblivious to the chill. I was pretty sure cigarettes were against camp policy. But I imagine counselors running around outdoors in their underwear and deserting their posts for hours at a time were too. Kyle seemed to have little use for the rules.

I strolled over to him. "What do you want, Kyle?"

He looked at me with a serious expression. "I don't want this Jimmy Warren business getting out of control."

I looked at him for a moment. "I'm glad to hear it. What do we do about it?"

"First, you need to leave Jimmy alone. He's had a hard time of it."

I wasn't sure I'd heard right. "What are you talking about?"

"Jimmy told me how you shoved him and threatened him last night."

I shook my head back and forth and said, "If Jimmy Warren told you that, then he was lying. If you bothered to ask any of the other boys about what happened, they'd tell you I didn't lay a finger on that kid and I didn't threaten him. I called him a little creep and told him not to disrespect my father again."

"So, you intimidated him?" Now there was a big word; not one I would have expected Kyle to know.

"Yeah, I intimidated him. So, what? That's the only language bullies like him understand."

"You shouldn't be picking on smaller kids."

"Jimmy is bigger than my brother," I said. "Last night, he shoved Randy into a ditch and you just stood there and watched him do it. After all, boys will be boys, you said. Now, you want to stand up for Jimmy?"

TWO DREAMS & OTHER TALES
Three Days at Sunset

"The two things are not the same."

"That's for damned sure! I didn't assault anyone and I'm not a stinking bully! Why do you defend Jimmy and not my brother? You say Jimmy's had a bad time. You think Randy hasn't? What do you have against him, anyway? Or is it me you don't like?"

Kyle knew he was losing control of the argument. He leaned closer and bared his teeth. "Just lay off the smaller kids."

"Kyle," I said, "if Jimmy Warren hurts Randy again, I'll make sure somebody around here deals with him. It would be better if it were you. I'm sure you don't want Coach hanging around when you're someplace you're not supposed to be." I could see in his eyes that he understood the implied threat. "I have another hour of sack time, so I'm going back to bed."

I walked back into the cabin. I got my own spare blanket out of my footlocker and laid it over Randy. I climbed back into my own bunk, but found I was too wound up to go back to sleep. That's just wonderful, I thought, with great annoyance. I hate starting the day in a bad mood. Such days only get worse as they progress.

***

It was 12:45 p.m. when our boys came out of the dining hall. As was our practice, we formed up two single-file lines and headed back to the cabin. Some might think this practice was a bit too rigid for a bunch of schoolboys at camp, but the lines were rarely straight and not too rigidly enforced. The idea was to maintain a level of order that assured we wouldn't have to go looking for boys who got separated from the group. At a camp with the number of boys we had, traffic control was a must.

Despite my fear of the day getting worse, it was a relatively quiet morning. Kyle said no more about our earlier conversation, though it still hung in the air between us. Randy declined the suggestion that we go see Coach about going home. I wasn't sure what had changed, but it seemed we had weathered our first crisis successfully. It was now midweek, and I hoped it would all be downhill from that point, but I doubted it.

TWO DREAMS & OTHER TALES
Three Days at Sunset

When we got to the admin building, Kyle told the boys to keep moving, but asked me to come inside with him. He explained he had staff meeting at 1:00 p.m. and would be back to the cabin later. Could I please keep an eye on things? Also, he wanted me to carry a bunch of paperwork back to the cabin and leave it on his bunk. It wasn't hard to do the math. Coach kept staff meetings to thirty minutes so that his counselors could get straight back to their unattended boys. If Kyle was coming back to the cabin later and wanted me to carry his paperwork for him, it was a good bet he planned to go somewhere else after the meeting. Apparently, my hint about Coach Morris that morning didn't have the effect I thought it had.

When I got back to the cabin, I didn't see any of our boys around. At first, I thought they were all inside, but then I heard a loud ruckus coming from out back. As I turned the corner into the backyard, I saw something I hadn't expected, but probably should have. I saw a group of eight boys shouting as they watched two others, Jimmy Warren and Eddie Baylor, working over my brother. Jimmy punched Randy in the stomach, causing him to double over. Before I could react, Eddie dropped to his hands and knees behind Randy and Jimmy gave Randy a shove, causing him to tumble backward over Eddie. Instead of hitting the ground cleanly, though, Randy's head struck the stone wall rather forcefully, causing him to land on the ground face down and unmoving. Rather than show any remorse or come to his aid, the two bullies jumped on Randy's back like buzzards on a carcass.

My blood boiled as I dropped Kyle's papers and ran across the yard toward the trouble. One of the assembled boys inadvertently stepped into my path and I plowed right through him. When I got to where Randy, Jimmy, and Eddie were, I grabbed Jimmy by both arms and dragged him to his feet. Before he knew what was happening, I sent him sprawling into the crowd of boys behind me. Eddie looked up at me just as I grabbed him the same way. A second later, he was sailing over the wall head first. Afraid that Randy was seriously injured, I turned him over and lifted his head from the ground.

"Randy, are you all right?" I asked.

"I'm fine," he said through clenched teeth.

TWO DREAMS & OTHER TALES
Three Days at Sunset

"Let me look at your head there."

As I reached in, he slapped my hand away and growled, "I told you I'm fine! Now get away from me!"

That was so unexpected that I stood up and stepped back, like I'd been shoved. Thinking maybe he just needed a minute to collect himself, I turned my attention to Jimmy Warren. "You get out of my sight!" Looking around, I saw Eddie Baylor slipping back over the wall, eyeing me fearfully. "You too!"

I looked at the rest of the boys, who were standing there open-mouthed. "All of you, take a hike right now!" They all quickly disappeared around the corner.

When I turned back to Randy, he was glaring at me. "Why did you do that?!"

"Do what?"

"Why did you break up that fight? Why didn't you mind your own business and let me finish this thing?"

"I don't understand," I said, confused. "Randy, you've never wanted to fight anybody before. Why now? Besides, that wasn't fighting. Those two almost put your lights out and then jumped on you when you were down. Why do you think I broke it up? Do you want to get beaten up?"

"No! But I don't want you saving me in front of everybody. Now they're all going to want to pick on me when you're not looking."

To me, this was amazingly grown-up talk for an eleven-year-old, especially my brother. But I also thought he was wrong. "Randy, except for Jimmy and Eddie, those boys aren't like that. They're your friends."

"Then why didn't *they* break it up? Why didn't *they* help me?"

I was stuck for an answer. I couldn't explain why boys that age would rather watch a fight than put a stop to it, even when a bully was involved, so I changed direction. "Randy, this wasn't a real fight. This was a couple of jerks being bullies. You know what Mom always tells you. Don't play the bully's game. Just walk away from them."

TWO DREAMS & OTHER TALES
Three Days at Sunset

"Walk away?!" Randy screamed. "Where am I supposed to go?! We're in the freakin' woods!" His outburst was rather frightening, as I had never seen such anger come out of him before. "I didn't want to come here, Luke. You and Mama made me come. Now go away and leave me alone!"

I stood there silently for a moment, then calmly said, "Randy, nobody made you come. Mom asked you to try this, and you said 'OK.' She asked me to come with you and I said 'OK.' We can still go talk to the coach. Nobody's going to make you stay."

Randy stared at the ground with an angry scowl and said nothing. I knew I wasn't going to get anywhere with him, so I walked over to where I'd drop Kyle's papers and scooped them up off the ground. I left the back yard and headed around to the front of the cabin. There I saw all the other boys, except Jimmy and Eddie, gathered in a group, whispering among themselves. I was certain they'd all overheard my argument with Randy, including the part where he suggested they weren't his friends. Denny Hillerman, the boy I shoved, came over to me. "Luke, we're really sorry about what happened back there. Is Randy OK?"

"Yeah, I think he'll be fine," I mumbled. "Everybody just leave him alone for the rest of the day." I looked all around me. "Where are Warren and Baylor?"

"They took off," Denny said, pointing down the camp road.

If I were the counselor, it would have been my job to go find them and bring them back. Forget that, I thought. They were Kyle's responsibility and if they got into mischief, they'd be *his* problem. I looked back at the group. They all seemed to be waiting for me to tell them what to do. "Kyle will be back in a while," I said. "We have the afternoon free until dinner, so do what you like. Just stay close by."

As the crowd broke up, I entered the cabin, dropped Kyle's stuff on his bunk, and laid down on my own. I tried to figure out who I'd just been arguing with. It wasn't the scared, timid child I grew up with. It certainly wasn't the hurt little boy who'd cried so hard on my shoulder the night before. The kid outside was possessed of an anger I'd never seen before, and a complete lack of fear. For a moment, I wondered if the impact of his

TWO DREAMS & OTHER TALES
Three Days at Sunset

head on that wall had caused some kind of damage, but I put that idea aside. The strangest part about the change in Randy was that it happened so suddenly. I finally decided to let the whole thing cool off and see how he was feeling at dinnertime. Maybe then the two of us would go see the coach about going home. If we did go home, I would have a lot of explaining to do.

Before long, the excitement died down and the boys got busy doing other things. A few of them were playing tag outside. A couple started a game of checkers there in the cabin. A couple more came in and laid out on their bunks like me. To them, it was just a lazy afternoon at camp. I tried to read a book I'd brought along, but couldn't keep my mind on it. Finally, I rolled over and drifted off to sleep.

***

I awoke with a start to a quiet room with half of our boys sacked out on their bunks. Judging by the sounds drifting in with the breeze, the rest were engaged in some loud outdoor activity. I looked at the clock on the wall and noted with alarm that it was 4:20 p.m. Not only had I slept for three hours, but we were about to be late for dinner! I sat up, jumped from my bunk, and started waking the boys, telling them to get up and come outside. I rushed out the door and began calling those out there to join me as well. Soon, everyone was assembled, except Randy and Kyle. Jimmy and Eddie were there, but keeping their distance.

"Guys," I said, "we're going to be late for dinner if we don't get going now. I don't know where Kyle is, so we'll just have to go without him."

Jeremy Parker stepped forward, grinning. "*We* know where Kyle is."

"Really? Where?"

Jeremy held out his hands in front of him like he was holding two large bags to his chest. The other boys giggled.

"Am I supposed to know what that means, Jeremy?"

The laughter got even louder. Jeremy said, "He's over at Camp Sunrise with his girlfriend. She's a counselor over there."

TWO DREAMS & OTHER TALES
Three Days at Sunset

"What girlfriend?"

He grinned again. "Caroline Becker, the blonde with the really big ones who doesn't wear a bra."

The laughter and noise were suddenly way too loud, so I waved for quiet. "Wait a minute, Jeremy. I know Caroline. She's not that—" I stopped abruptly and paused to think. "I think you're exaggerating a bit and that bra thing isn't true."

Timmy Mathis jumped in. "Yes, it is. Everyone can tell." All the other boys laughed, and some nodded in agreement.

Having once had a dirty little mind of my own, I knew they wouldn't let it go if I didn't move the discussion along, so I asked, "How do you all know her? And how do you know she's a counselor over there?"

Jeremy said, "She hangs out with Kyle at the Youth Center sometimes. She was on the bus with us coming here on Sunday. They were in the back seat and you wouldn't believe what they were doing."

Now I felt sure he was exaggerating. Not even Kyle was brazen enough to do whatever Jeremy was talking about on a bus with Coach Morris aboard—and a bunch of preadolescent boys watching.

"I'm sure you guys think this is funny," I said, "but it's not, OK? If Kyle gets caught messing around over at the other camp, Coach will bounce him out of here. Without a counselor, they'll break us up or send us home. You guys be careful what you say about this when Coach is around. Don't lie, but don't tell him if he doesn't ask. We'll get along without Kyle when he isn't here. OK?"

The laughter died again, and they all looked very serious. I forcefully repeated, "OK?" They nodded. By tossing out this command and extracting agreement, I had effectively taken over Kyle's job, which I'd been doing for much of the week, anyway.

As the boys formed up two lines to head for the dining hall, I looked around. "Has anyone seen Randy?"

TWO DREAMS & OTHER TALES
Three Days at Sunset

Andy Withers, an eleven-year-old, spoke up. "He's been out behind the cabin by himself all afternoon."

I told everyone to wait, then circled around the cabin. Randy was sitting on the wall staring at the ground. I walked over to him. "Randy, we've got to go to dinner now."

"I'm not hungry," he said in a grumpy tone.

"Randy, you know the rules. You can't be here by yourself. You have to come with us."

"I don't want to eat with them!"

"You don't have to eat with them! You can sit anywhere you like in the dining hall or outside. But you are coming with us, so get up."

Randy looked up, then stared at me for several seconds.

"Come on," I said firmly.

He jumped to his feet, huffed, and stomped past me. "There, are you happy now?"

I looked off into the woods, shaking my head back and forth. "Not really," I whispered.

***

Randy rediscovered his appetite, but sat by himself across the room. Some of our boys commented to me about it, but most of them paid the situation no mind. I saw Jimmy Warren and Eddie Baylor watching him and talking in whispers, no doubt planning some new mischief. I finished eating first and carried my dinner tray to the collection window. As I headed back to the table, Coach Morris approached.

"Hello, Luke," he said, "How is it going?"

I hesitated, then said without conviction, "All right, I guess."

He didn't seem to think so. "I see your brother sitting on the other side of the room, away from everybody. Is your group having some kind of problem?"

TWO DREAMS & OTHER TALES
Three Days at Sunset

The coach had always been very perceptive. Leave it to him to notice something like that. Before I could think it through, I said, "Yes, sir. We had trouble up at our cabin today." I described Randy's bully problem and told him about the fight and the fallout.

At my third mention of Jimmy, Coach said, "The Warren kid, huh? Now, there's a difficult case. We've been working with him a lot at the Youth Center, but he needs a lot more help than we're equipped to give." The coach stopped, checked himself, and lowered his voice. "The father is a violent man and Jimmy has been on the receiving end of a lot of it." Leaning closer, he whispered, "That's no secret, but it's not a subject for loose talk, either. OK?"

Suddenly, things that both Kyle and Jimmy had said to me made sense. "No wonder Jimmy hates his father so much," I said. I related his 'I hate the bastard' remark from the night before. "I'm sure I didn't help by bragging about *my* father. I suppose I should stop doing that."

"Luke, you're proud of your father and you have every reason to be. You don't have to apologize to anybody for that pride."

"Thanks, Coach. My biggest problem now is that I'm not sure what to do with Randy. I don't understand his behavior at all. He's always relied on me and now he's mad at me for protecting him. Do you understand that?"

"I think I might. In my years of teaching, I've seen many bullying situations. Sometimes bullies grow out of it, get put in their place, or grow into adult bullies and end up in trouble with the law. With the victims, it's different. Sometimes, we aren't even aware of them. Even when we are, some are too scared to make an issue of it. On rare occasions, you get the desperate one who brings a weapon to school or commits suicide. Thankfully, our school hasn't had any cases like that. Then you get some who reach their limit and say, 'I'm not taking it anymore,' and fight back."

"Do you think my brother is one of those?" I asked.

"If this is a sudden change of attitude, as you say, then that would be my guess. After everything else, maybe he's just had enough."

TWO DREAMS & OTHER TALES
Three Days at Sunset

"My dad always told him to stand up for himself. But I didn't see this coming. So, what should I do? Stand by and let them fight?"

Coach took a deep breath. "Remember two things," he said. "First, I'm responsible to the parents for the safety of their kids. I can't sanction fighting and if my staff sees it, they have to stop it and report it. Second, dealing with this problem isn't *your* job, it's Kyle's. What is *he* doing about it?"

I hesitated, then said, "Ignoring it. He doesn't think it's a problem, just a case of boys being boys. He thinks I'm making too much of it."

"Well, if we have boys getting hurt, then this needs to be dealt with. I think we'll take this matter up at the next staff meeting. By the way, where was Kyle when this was going on today?"

I realized my mistake. I was on the verge of doing what I told the other boys not to do: giving Coach enough information to suspect Kyle had been AWOL. Fortunately, the truth gave nothing away this time. I told him Kyle was at the staff meeting.

"What did he do about it when he got back?"

I hesitated again. "He ran off to deal with something else this afternoon. He never had the chance to do anything about it." Though this was also a true statement, I felt guilty about it because it was misleading. I'd once been taught that a lie of omission is a sin. I couldn't say for certain where Kyle had been all afternoon, but I had a good idea.

Coach looked over at our table. "You don't know where Kyle is now, do you?"

I pointed at the serving line. "He's right over there."

Kyle had come in the side door while we were talking and rushed over to the serving line, no doubt hoping to get something to eat before they closed. I'm sure he was also hoping Coach Morris wouldn't notice that he had just arrived from parts unknown. Coach turned to him and they eyed one another for a couple of seconds. He then looked at his watch and said, "Your bunch is going to be late for the archery range if you don't move now. I'm afraid Kyle will have to pass on seconds tonight. Why don't you roust your boys and I'll tell him?"

When I walked away from the coach, I was unsure of myself. I should have told him the whole truth and let him deal with Kyle. Part of my reason for not doing so was the schoolboy code. Even at my age, it was understood that if you ratted out a mate, you became a snitch and an outcast in the eyes of others. But the main reason was the one I gave the boys: if Kyle got bounced, we might all end up paying for his misdeeds.

As the boys lined up outside to head for the archery range, Kyle came out of the building. Judging by his look, I assumed he was unhappy about the prospect of going to bed without his supper. As we started down the trail, he grabbed my elbow and pulled me out of line. We were walking slower than the other boys and they started pulling away from us. He spoke with menace in his voice. "What was that all about in there?"

"What was what?" I asked innocently.

"What were you talking to Coach Morris about?"

"Not that you care, but we were talking about my brother."

He rolled his eyes. "Not that Jimmy Warren thing again? Why are you so wound up about that? And why are you bringing Coach into it? Don't you know the problems that can cause for me?"

I stopped walking, then turned and faced him. "What makes you think I care about *your* troubles, Kyle? And I didn't bring Coach into it. He asked me why Randy was eating alone, so I told him about the trouble at the cabin today."

Kyle gave me a puzzled look. "What trouble?"

"Exactly, Kyle. You don't know about the trouble because you weren't there. Warren and Baylor tried to beat up Randy. They slammed his head against that stone wall behind the cabin. Randy could have been seriously hurt and you would have been blamed for it because you weren't doing your job. Then, you'd have to tell Coach where you've been sneaking off to all week."

TWO DREAMS & OTHER TALES
Three Days at Sunset

His eyes grew wide and there was alarm in his voice. "You didn't tell him where I was, did you?"

"I told him you were at staff meeting, which you were. I didn't tell him where you went after that because I don't know where you keep going." I hesitated. "But the other boys in our cabin think they know."

Kyle gave me another puzzled look. "Why? What did they say?"

I smirked and said, "They told me Caroline Becker doesn't wear a bra."

Kyle balled his right hand into a fist and turned red in the face. "That's not funny, Dillard!" he shouted.

"That's what I told *them*," I said. "And don't worry about Randy; he's just fine. Thanks for asking."

Without another word, I turned and trotted off to catch up with our boys. I didn't hear Kyle's footsteps behind me, so I assumed he wasn't following close, if at all. I thought about it for a bit and decided it was just as well that I told him. If Kyle was sneaking over to Camp Sunrise, he now knew his secret was out and that the boys he was in charge of regarded him as a joke. Maybe that would change his behavior, benefiting us all.

After our time at the archery range, we returned to the dining hall for movie night. They were playing an old Disney comedy about a Volkswagen beetle with a mind of its own and a habit of getting into mischief. Randy was still in a sullen mood, but had rejoined his mates—avoiding Warren, Baylor, and me. I watched as Kyle went back for seconds and then thirds on popcorn. I suppose that's what happens when you don't eat dinner. If I ate that much popcorn on an empty stomach and washed it down with soda pop, I'd have been sick as a dog.

THURSDAY

We had a thunderstorm and heavy rain on Thursday morning before daylight. Though the overcast was already clearing off at sunrise, it would be wet and muddy around camp for most of the day. I awoke about thirty minutes before reveille and turned over. The first thing I noticed was that Randy's bunk was empty. I sat up and looked around the room, but nobody else was up yet and the bathroom was dark. Something told me I should get up and go look for my brother.

I climbed out of my own bunk and quickly dressed. I headed out the cabin door and made a complete circuit of the building, but Randy wasn't around. I looked up and down the camp road, wondering which direction he had gone. Instinct told me to go toward the center of the camp. I walked that way, wondering what Randy's mood was going to be like. When I reached the small admin building, I saw Coach Morris standing on the front porch, drinking from a coffee mug. When he saw me, he pointed toward the waterfront and said, "Your brother went that way."

"Thanks, Coach," I mumbled.

"Is everything all right this morning?"

"I don't know, sir. I guess I'll find out."

When I got to the waterfront area, I saw Randy sitting on the edge of the pier about halfway down. He was dressed in khaki shorts and a white t-shirt. His sneakers sat on the pier while his feet were submerged in the water. As I approached, he looked up and saw me coming. His jaw tightened, and he looked away, making it clear he wasn't happy to see me.

"Randy, are you OK?" I asked. He said nothing, so I waited a moment.

"How long are you going to stay mad at me?" He still said nothing.

"Aren't you going to say something? Like, good morning, at least?" He still didn't speak.

"Fine, have it your way." I turned and stomped off down the pier. I only made it about ten feet onto the shore when I stopped and looked back. I couldn't walk away with things like this. I turned and rushed back to him.

"Dammit, Randy!" I shouted. "You're my little brother and I love you. There, I said it." I choked back my emotions and continued. "The day we buried Dad, I stood at his grave and promised him I would take care of you and Mom. I promised Mom the same thing the day we came to camp. When I saw you hit your head on that wall yesterday, I was scared. I was afraid you were badly hurt, and I didn't know what I was going to tell Mom. When those boys wouldn't get off you, I got mad and pulled them off. I'm not going to say I'm sorry for what I did, because I'm not. I'm your big brother and protecting you is my job." I still got no response, so I turned and walked away, feeling defeated.

I was halfway back to the admin building when I heard fast footsteps crunching the gravel behind me and Randy calling, "Luke, wait up." I turned to see him running awkwardly, his sneakers unlaced and partially soaked because they had wet feet in them. When he caught up to me, I could tell he was fighting back tears. He looked at the ground and mumbled, "I'm sorry I got mad."

"Randy, look at me, please." Slowly, he looked up. "I didn't say I was sorry, so you don't have to either. I know you were mad because you wanted to stand up for yourself and I got in the way. But you were in more trouble than you thought you were. Those boys were fighting dirty and I couldn't just stand by and watch. I don't know what to do about them without making trouble for all of us. But somehow, we'll figure it out together. You trust me, don't you?" He shook his head up and down.

I stepped closer, dropped to one knee, and began tying his shoelaces. When I stood up again, I reached out, took his hand, and said, "I never knew you were so hard-headed."

I was pretty sure he didn't understand my double meaning, but he laughed with me, anyway. We turned and started up the road together. The coach smiled and waved as we passed the admin building again. I returned both the smile and the wave. We had now survived our second crisis, and I had my little brother back. I couldn't help wondering, though, how long it would take for Jimmy Warren to screw it up again.

***

After breakfast, we spent the morning watching demonstrations and lectures given by officers from our own town police department. The boys were most engaged while watching a police K-9 officer put his dog through the paces. Naturally, this bunch of preadolescent boys were most interested in hearing about car chases and shootouts, but were disappointed to learn that everyday police work wasn't as exciting as all that. In fact, one officer assured us that a shooting situation was the last place any police officer wanted to find him or herself. Thinking of my father, I felt certain a lot of military types felt the same way.

After lunch, we all got into swim trunks and headed down to the lake for afternoon free swim. When we got there, Kyle headed for No Man's Land again. Unbelievable, I thought. Even with the threat of exposure hanging over him, he just couldn't stay away. Randy sat on the sand with me for most of the time and watched the others. Some boys—egged on by Warren and Baylor—teased him for not being able to swim. Randy closed down and tuned them out. We got back up to the cabin just before 3:45 p.m. and changed out of our swim clothes. By the time I finished changing, all the other boys had already gone back outdoors.

As I was coming out of the cabin, I heard a loud uproar coming from out back. Not again, I thought to myself. Even before I got around to the far side of the building, I knew what I was going to see. Unfolding right there before me was a repeat of the scene from the previous day. I saw my brother struggling to get free of Eddie Baylor, who had his arms pinned, while Jimmy Warren was trying to throw a punch at him. A low growl was coming out of Randy's mouth, but it was mostly drowned out by Jimmy shouting.

"Hold him, Eddie! Hold him still!"

I ran toward the action. Jimmy had his back to me, while Randy and Eddie were facing in my direction. Eddie saw me first and quickly let go of Randy. Released without warning, Randy's arms started flailing. Jimmy, who hadn't seen me yet, shouted, "What did you let go for?!"

Suddenly, everyone was aware of my presence and everything just seemed to stop. Jimmy turned and looked at me with defiance, but said nothing. Randy looked at me with obvious frustration. As much as I hated the idea of him fighting, I decided it was time to let him decide for himself what he would do. But first, I was going to level the playing field.

"What's going on, Warren?" I asked.

He tried to sound like an adult. "Nothing. Randy and I are just settling things."

TWO DREAMS & OTHER TALES
Three Days at Sunset

I shook my head. "What did my brother do to you that needs to be settled? And how does having Baylor hold him while you punch him settle it? You're both bigger than he is, so it looks like plain old bullying to me. Nobody likes a bully."

To my surprise, there was a murmur of agreement from the assembled group of boys. That's one for our side, I thought.

"Yeah?" Jimmy said. "What are you going to do about it? Are you going to hurt me?"

I chuckled. "No, Jimmy, I'm not going to hurt you. I get it now. You both have something to prove. You want to beat up a smaller boy to show the others how tough you are, and Randy doesn't want to hide behind me. Sooner or later, you two are going to fight no matter what I say. So, I'll stay out of the way—on one condition."

Jimmy and Randy both stared at me, no doubt wondering what was coming. I said, "Eddie Baylor is going to sit this one out and you're going to give my brother a fair fight."

Jimmy considered that for a few seconds. "And if I don't?"

"Then I'll put you in a headlock and send for Coach Morris. Or you could just walk away. What's it going to be?"

Jimmy looked at the other boys. He could walk away, but he'd lose face. If I did what I threatened, he'd lose his dignity and end up in trouble. If he fought fair, Randy might give him a real fight. It was a case of choosing the lesser evil. Finally, he said, "OK. Eddie sits out."

Without another word, I turned my glare on Eddie Baylor, who hurried out of the way. I took Randy by the shoulder, spun him around, and walked him to the far end of the clearing. I lowered my voice and asked him, "Do you really want to do this?"

He looked down at his feet. "Nope."

"But you're going to do it, anyway?"

"Yup."

"You understand why I'm not happy about it?"

TWO DREAMS & OTHER TALES
Three Days at Sunset

"Yup."

"If you go home all bruised up from fighting, Mom will kick both of our tails."

He looked up. "I'm sorry."

"You don't have to be sorry. I'm letting you decide. But if that creep is going to get us both in trouble, you make him pay for it. Remember, he's a bully, and if you give him a real fight, he can't win, even if he beats you silly."

He nodded and said, "OK."

"Now listen," I said. "He's taller than you are and has longer arms. If he can keep away from you, he can hit you all day without you hitting him back. You need to rush him and get in close before he's ready. Understand?"

"Yup."

"Good." I patted his shoulder. "Show him that messing with Randy Dillard was a big mistake."

As I moved to where the other boys were standing, I told myself that this was a stupid idea. It felt like I had let my brother down, promising to help him find a solution to the problem, then standing quietly by until it blew up again. Now, Randy would solve it Jimmy's way, without my help. No matter how it ended, I knew my mother would probably punish me severely—and I would deserve it.

Randy walked straight toward Jimmy, stopping just out of his reach. They stared each other down for a moment. Just as Jimmy raised his fists, Randy charged him. He didn't even get off a punch before Randy crashed into him shoulder-first, causing him to lose balance. He fell over backward, with Randy on top. What followed for the next couple of minutes was more of a wrestling match than a fistfight. They grappled and rolled about on the muddy ground, each one tossing a few punches. Only two connected: one hit Jimmy in the right eye; the other caught Randy square on the jaw. Through it all, the rest of the boys shouted and cheered.

TWO DREAMS & OTHER TALES
Three Days at Sunset

As suddenly as it started, it was over. The two boys lay on their backs side-by-side, exhausted, both gasping for breath and covered with mud. Rather than let either of them get their second wind and start again, I stepped in. "OK, boys, I think we're finished here." I looked back at the crowd and said, "Looks like a draw to me, guys. Everyone agree?" They all nodded. I grabbed hold of Jimmy's arm and pulled him to his feet, then turned and did the same with Randy. "OK, fellas. Clean yourselves off and let's go get ready for dinner."

As the two boys were pulling themselves together, Kyle Weston appeared from around the corner of the cabin. He took one look at Jimmy and Randy, disheveled and muddy, and asked, "What the hell is going on here?" Everyone looked at him, but nobody said anything. "What's going on?" Pointing at me, he said, "Dillard, these two have been fighting. Did you put them up to this?"

I threw up my hands and spoke in an exaggerated tone. "Not me, boss. I've been doing what you said: letting the boys be boys. Sometimes they argue, make faces, and even fight. This time, they both kicked butt, and you missed it."

"You're not supposed to be letting them fight!"

I pointed my finger at him. "No, Kyle! *You* are the one who's not supposed to be letting them fight. *You* are supposed to be in charge here, not me. If you were here doing what you're supposed to do, it probably wouldn't have come to this."

Kyle stepped within striking distance of me, red in the face. "I'm getting tired of you telling me how to do my job, Dillard."

"And I'm getting tired of doing your job for you while you get paid for it," I yelled back. "Why don't you go back over to Camp Sunrise and play with your girlfriend some more? We don't need your lazy butt around here."

Kyle grabbed me by the collar and slammed me into the wall of the cabin. I banged my head and everything got slightly blurry. He pressed his left hand against my chest and reared back to hit me with a closed fist. Despite his exhaustion, Randy launched himself at Kyle and jumped onto

TWO DREAMS & OTHER TALES
Three Days at Sunset

his back. As Kyle swung around trying to get him off, a loud, shrill noise split the air. Then, everything stopped. We all turned to the source of that sound and there stood Coach Herman Morris, his coach's whistle still in his mouth. If looks could kill, Kyle Weston would have dropped dead right there on the spot.

Coach let the whistle drop from his mouth. "Mr. Weston, front and center, now!!" Kyle shook loose from Randy and hastened over to the coach, looking at him with obvious fear. Coach angrily said, "It seems like every time I've seen this bunch the last couple of days, you were almost never with them. Twice this week, you've been late for staff meeting and today, you missed it completely. A short while ago, Mrs. Donovan called from the other camp to tell me that an unidentified boy was spotted over there today. When you came hot-footing it past my office a few minutes ago, I finally put it together. I came up to look things over and I'm not sure which upsets me more: seeing you assault one of my boys, or learning that my suspicions about you are correct. You and I are going to deal with this in my office at the Youth Center on Monday morning. You be there at 9:00 a.m. and bring a parent. Understood?"

Kyle spoke with little more than a whisper. "Yes, sir."

Coach continued. "In the meantime, there's a bus back to the Youth Center leaving the parking lot in about twenty minutes. Pack your gear and be on it." Kyle stared at him for a moment, waiting to be dismissed. "Move!!" He disappeared around the corner.

All was quiet for a minute as the coach stood there staring at the ground, obviously fuming. Finally, he gave me a come-here gesture and said, "Mr. Dillard." I walked over to him with all the boys crowding in behind me. "Are you OK, son?"

"Yes, Coach. No damage done."

"Good boy. Luke, I just created a problem for myself. We're understaffed already and now I'm short one counselor. For liability reasons, I have to have one for each cabin. Since we're full up, I only have two choices: send you all home with Kyle, which would hardly be fair, or move in here myself and be your counselor—on paper, at least. I have too many other duties to be here most of the time, which means I'll need to leave one of you in charge during the day. I hope I can get away with that." He paused again, then continued. "This group always seems to be in good order when I see them and you seem to be the one keeping that order, not Kyle. Do you think you could handle it if I left you in charge here? It would be for less than two days."

"Yes, sir, I can do that." The boys buzzed with excitement. I turned and held up my hand until they were quiet again.

Coach grinned. "It looks to me like you're in charge already. Now, I can't put you on the payroll, so this will be a favor to me. And I always repay favors generously."

"Thank you, sir."

"You won't have to attend staff meetings, but when you finish dinner tonight, please come by my table so we can chat."

Coach took a long look at our group of boys. His gaze lingered a few extra seconds on Randy and Jimmy. I'm sure it was rather obvious to him what had been going on before he and Kyle arrived. He pulled me aside and asked in a hushed tone, "May I assume that your brother and the Warren kid have taken care of their problem?"

I hesitated, then grinned. "Yes, sir. I think it's all settled now."

He stared at me for a moment, clearly undecided on what to say next. Policy required him to take a hard stand on the matter, but he'd already thrown the rule book away—and put himself at risk by doing so.

Finally, he smiled. "Good man. For obvious reasons, I don't want to know the details. I'll see you at dinner."

The boys cheered as he disappeared around the corner of the cabin. I waved for quiet. "Listen, guys. We need to leave for dinner in ten minutes. Since Coach is moving in and we may get inspected tonight or tomorrow, let's take a few minutes to straighten up the cabin. OK?" They all nodded agreement.

Three Days at Sunset

As they started for the front door, I pulled Randy and Jimmy aside. "Guys, do you think we can have peace now?" They both nodded. "Show me." Randy held out his hand and Jimmy slapped it. "No, I mean for real." Jimmy took Randy's hand and shook it.

I said to Jimmy, "Can you make sure Baylor understands about the truce?"

"Yup."

"And Jimmy, I hope what I said the other night wasn't too hurtful. If it was, I'm sorry."

He looked at his feet and mumbled, "I'm sorry about your dad," then turned and ran after the other boys.

I looked at Randy, but before I could speak, he threw himself at me, wrapping his muddy arms around me. I put mine around him as well and we stood like that for a minute. He let go, stepped back, and looked up at me with tears running down each of his dirty cheeks.

"Thanks, Luke," he said.

"You're going to be OK, little brother. We're both going to be OK now."

That was the last time I ever saw my brother cry.

Arlington National Cemetery
Virginia, July 2008

The sound of the last volley echoed across the open ground. As the notes of taps were played by the bugler, my memory lingered a moment longer on that summer and what followed. In the wake of his battle with Jimmy Warren, Randy underwent a transformation that was immediate, complete, and somewhat startling. He no longer slouched when he walked or stared at the ground when talking to others. He stood up straight and strode like a man with purpose. He looked everyone in the eye when he talked to them and spoke directly and firmly. Rather than hide from adversity, he stood up for himself when trouble arose. As he got older, he also got taller, leaner, and stronger. His peers came to understand that Randy

TWO DREAMS & OTHER TALES
Three Days at Sunset

Dillard wasn't someone to mess with. In high school, he excelled academically, and I believe, would have done well in college. However, my brother chose the same path our father took. He spent his first summer out of school in basic training at Parris Island and came home a US Marine. That was the same year I graduated from ROTC at Ohio State and began my own military career as a Navy ensign.

The casket team executed the very meticulous procedure for flourishing, stretching, folding, and passing the flag that had adorned Randy's casket. The folding action turned it into a triangular object which bore a slight resemblance to a dark blue bicorne hat adorned with white stars. The officer-in-charge came around the casket to where my mother was sitting and I was standing. He bent down before Mom and placed the flag in her hands, saying, "On behalf of the President of the United States and the people of a grateful nation, may I present this flag as a token of appreciation for the honorable and faithful service your loved one has rendered this nation?"

He straightened up and saluted her, turned and exchanged salutes with me, then spun on his heels and marched away. Next came a senior Marine Corps officer who was there to offer condolences on behalf of the Commandant. I exchanged salutes with him, then stood at attention while he spoke briefly with my mother. He then extended his hand to me, telling me that the Corps was extremely proud of my brother and his seventeen years of service to the nation.

After he was gone, I sat back down with Mom and placed my arm around her. She was staring at the flag in her lap, no doubt remembering the last time she'd been through this experience. Twice in one lifetime just didn't seem fair. After a short interval, Mom rose from her seat and I rose with her. She clutched the flag to her chest with her left hand, while in her right was the single long-stemmed white rose she had been holding since we arrived. She stepped forward and placed the flower on the casket. She then kissed her fingertips and touched them to it.

"Goodbye, my sweet little one," she said. "Take good care of your daddy." She turned to me and said in a strained voice, "Luke, please make me a promise."

TWO DREAMS & OTHER TALES
Three Days at Sunset

"Anything, Mom."

"Promise me I won't have to bury you, too. I couldn't live through this a third time, especially if I had to do it alone."

What could I say? As an active-duty military man, I couldn't truthfully promise not to die on duty. That is the cost of defending one's country sometimes. But how could a good son say no to his grieving mother?

"I promise, Mom. No more burials."

With that promise made and received, Mom collapsed into my arms and wept bitterly. Until that moment, I never understood the burden she carried all those years. She had once been the long-suffering wife of a fighting Marine. Then, for the sake of her children, she wore the face of a brave Marine widow. Then it all began again. For seventeen years, she was the worried mother of two military sons, one of whom joined the Marines and deployed to the same war zone three times. Now, the cycle was complete once more as she laid her youngest to rest in this most hallowed of places.

However, the cycle of pride, worry, and grief were more complicated for her than I ever realized. That night, she told me for the first time that her deepest regret had come not from seeing her men off to war, but from the way she sent her youngest son away to summer camp when he was eleven years old. That puzzled me at first, but then she elaborated. She said that when she put us on the bus to camp that day, she did not know the scared little boy she was sending away would return a completely different child. Had she known, she would have given him a proper goodbye. She would have held him a little tighter for just a little longer and told him how very much she loved him. My mother was proud of the man Randy became, but secretly, she grieved for the needy child she lost that summer. She could never say anything like that in front of him, though, for fear he might take it as a rebuke. Now that he was at peace and beyond caring, Mom could openly grieve for both of her lost sons: the fallen Marine who lost his life on a foreign battlefield; and the sweet, timid little boy who never came home from Camp Sunset.

TWO DREAMS & OTHER TALES
Three Days at Sunset

TALE #5. MY FATHER'S PROMISE

December 1941

Has someone ever described to you an experience they've had that defies explanation? Like the person sensing unseen danger or misfortune and acting to escape or somehow avert it? Or sensing the need of another person and addressing it before being told about it? Or seeking someone or something that was lost and somehow knowing exactly where to look? I've heard many such stories. In fact, most families I know have at least one such story in their lore. My family has one too, except that ours is not about a sudden feeling or revelation followed by some kind of decisive action. It's more like a prophecy played out over two decades against the backdrop of an eventful stretch of American and world history. As dubious as that claim sounds, it really is quite a story. To tell it, I suppose I should start at the beginning.

Our president called it a day that shall live in infamy, and he was right. Anybody who remembers that Sunday in December 1941 could tell you where they were and what they were doing when they learned of the Japanese attack on Pearl Harbor. It is a seminal moment forever engraved on the consciousness of our nation. I was very young at the time and don't remember Pearl Harbor very well. That month, my focus was on Christmas—in particular, Christmas Eve, which was to be my seventh birthday. What I do remember about that month was how our family time suddenly became more rushed and more precious. What I remember much more clearly than December 7 was Monday, March 2, 1942, three months after Pearl Harbor—the day my father left home for the war in Europe. I remember it particularly well because it was the last time I ever saw him.

Life quickly changed in the U.S. Young men rushed to the recruiting offices to join up. Women began going to work in large numbers. War bonds were on sale—I didn't know what those were. Shortages and rationing suddenly became a way of life as America began to prepare for the long fight and the lean years ahead.

TWO DREAMS & OTHER TALES
My Father's Promise

My father, Jim Pearson, Sr., had a skill our country would need in great abundance: he was a military pilot. He had been a U.S. Army officer for ten years and trained as a bomber pilot, primarily on the B-17 Flying Fortress, while achieving the rank of captain. That December, he'd been out of the military for less than a year, flying passenger service for a regional airline. In January, they recalled him to duty, recertifying him and training him on the B-25 Mitchell. By the end of his training, he knew he was going to Europe to fight Germans.

That Monday morning, we gathered with the families of other airmen to say goodbye. My mother, Helen, was sobbing as she had been for several days. She feared Dad would go missing in combat and never return. As he prepared to leave, she clung to him. Looking into her red, swollen eyes, he uttered the words that haunt me to this day. "Don't worry, dear," he said, "I'll be home for Christmas."

To anyone with knowledge of the world situation, such words would have sounded like nonsense. The Japanese and Germans had had plenty of time to fortify their positions. To uproot them and send them back where they belonged would take years. It was unlikely that anyone, except the dead and disabled, would come home by Christmas that year. But to a seven-year-old boy, the words carried the force of a sacred promise. From that point on, I marked time by asking my mother how long it was until Christmas. I asked with the firm belief that when she finally announced its arrival, the war would be over, and my father would be home.

Mom never learned a lot about what Dad was doing, but she assumed he was flying bombing missions over Germany. She didn't know how many missions he flew or how dangerous it was. She would only tell me he was keeping busy with the war. His early letters arrived heavily censored by a hand other than his own. As he and his mates soon learned, their letters home had to be carefully worded so as not to compromise the security of their mission. His letters became little more than greeting cards, assuring us that he was well and that he still loved us very much. Unfortunately, they said little else.

You cannot imagine how bitterly disappointed I was when Christmas 1942 came and went with no appearance by my father and no

TWO DREAMS & OTHER TALES
My Father's Promise

mention of any return in his letters. When the following Christmas passed the same way, my disappointment turned to disillusionment. I couldn't understand why Dad made such a critical promise if he wouldn't—or couldn't—keep it. Maybe telling us when he would finally come home was one of those things they wouldn't allow him to share in his letters.

The year 1944 brought many significant changes. Even someone my age could sense from the talk of others that the war was turning our way. After D-Day in June, many began to express hope that the war would finally come to an end. Unfortunately, that enthusiasm was short-lived at our house. That month, word came from the Army that Dad and his crew had gone missing. They vanished from the face of the earth during a bad weather mission. We waited for word that they were prisoners or that someone found the wreckage of their plane. Weeks passed, then months, with no word—there was nothing to tell.

It was difficult dealing with the reactions of those around us. When the fallen came home for burial, the community would gather around their families and grieve with them. This was true even for those lost or buried at sea, or interred in some foreign place. It was a different story for those missing in action. What do you say to the family of one whose fate is unknown? Do you encourage them to grieve as though their beloved were dead? Or do you tell them to have faith and believe in a positive outcome? Many family friends, uncertain of what to say, kept their distance. With her worst fear realized, my mother fell into long bouts of silence. For me, the loss and almost certain death of my dad was a wound that would not heal, and my tears were bitter ones.

The war ended in the summer of 1945. The veterans came home, and the community celebrated, but not me. My dad promised to come home for Christmas, but never came home at all. Life went on for everyone else, including my mother it seemed. After a period of several months, her veil of grief lifted, replaced by a sort of devil-may-care attitude. I recognized it for the first time during the fall of that year. Experiencing extreme frustration over a school project determined to go wrong, I said aloud for the first time, "I wish Daddy were here."

TWO DREAMS & OTHER TALES
My Father's Promise

Without missing a beat, my smiling mother said, "Don't worry, dear, your father will be home for Christmas."

I thought I'd misunderstood and asked her to repeat what she said. She said it again with complete sincerity. I was ten years old and didn't know what to think. My father couldn't still be alive, could he? During the next several years, she made the same declaration again and again. When some problem arose and I complained to her about it, she'd assure me my father would come home at Christmas and make everything right. That never made me feel better and never gave me reason for hope. Each time, it was like having salt poured into an open wound. As I grew older and my thought processes matured, I came to believe my mother had something wrong with her. The only reason I didn't tell her she was crazy was because my father once punished me for being disrespectful to her. However, my patience was not unlimited, and it was running out.

It came to a head when I was sixteen. One day, my mother once again cheerfully told me my father would be home for Christmas and my frustration boiled over.

"What year?" I demanded.

She looked at me, stunned. "I beg your pardon."

"For years, you've been telling me my dead father is coming home for Christmas! Christmas comes every year, so what year are you talking about?"

She stared at me for a few more seconds, then her face became a mask of grief. She burst into tears and fled from the room. Few things could reduce me to shame more than my mother crying over something I'd done. But on that occasion, my shame was mixed with a dose of defiance. If we weren't going to address my father's death, then I didn't want to talk about him at all.

I got some of my wish, but I ended up sorry for it. Dad became a forbidden subject, as Mom would no longer talk to me about him. It was like he never existed. She also stopped celebrating Christmas. Each December, she would go into a serious bout of depression and ship me off to celebrate the holiday and my birthday with my father's relatives.

TWO DREAMS & OTHER TALES
My Father's Promise

Despite the growing distance between us, she was still a very concerned mother. Our country went to war again in 1950, this time on the Korean Peninsula. Mom always worried when the war news came on. She feared I would get drafted into the Army and end up in combat like my father. Since I was an only son, that wasn't likely, but one could never tell in wartime. After I graduated high school in 1953, I did go into the Army and spent a year overseas, though the fighting in Korea was already over. I spent the rest of my enlistment on an Army base in the States.

After my two-year hitch, I went to school, taking advantage of my G. I. Bill. I got my degree and took a job in a nearby city. In 1956, I voted in my first presidential election, and like most of America, I liked Ike. I also married a woman named Rachel, who was an angel—at least she was *my* angel. During the next few years, we bought a house and had two children, James—named for Dad and myself—and Elizabeth. I was a doting father, and they were my pride and joy.

Through all of this, my relationship with my mother remained strained. We kept in touch, but it was infrequent. It was always cordial, but reserved. She wanted to be close to her grandchildren, but did her best not to show it. Rachel, who lost her parents early in life, wanted to be close to my mother, but the state of my relationship with her made that difficult. She didn't understand because I had never told her the story of my father's parting words and the problems they caused.

It was during the Christmas season of 1961 when it all came out. I startled Rachel one night by loudly refusing to sing *I'll Be Home for Christmas* with her and some friends. She demanded to know why I was so hard to live with every holiday season, so I told her. After learning the whole story, she became determined to bring Mom and me back together. She claimed it was for the children's sake, but I knew it was for my benefit as well. She invited Mom for Christmas, and to my surprise, my mother agreed to come.

It would have been a delightful holiday for all of us if Mom hadn't fallen ill. It wasn't just some simple bug, either; something was seriously wrong. I forgot all the problems we had between us as I became consumed with worry about her health. The day after Christmas, I called her doctor

TWO DREAMS & OTHER TALES
My Father's Promise

and then, following his direction, took her to the hospital where she underwent a battery of tests. On New Year's Day, we sat in a consulting room with a young doctor who seemed ill at ease and who clearly had bad news. Rather than get straight to the diagnosis and prognosis, he started with a very technical explanation of the tests performed.

My no-nonsense mother finally interrupted. "Let's get to the point, Doctor. What's wrong with me?"

He hesitated and took a deep breath. "You have cancer, Mrs. Pearson."

Mom accepted that news calmly. The doctor explained the type of cancer she had, that it was inoperable, and that it would be terminal. For medical science, understanding and beating cancer was still a long way off. The clinical nature of his discourse couldn't mask the genuine emotion beneath the surface. You would have thought he'd never delivered this news before. He told us with a tremble in his voice how very sorry he was.

Without giving him a chance to collect himself, Mom asked, "How long do I have?"

"Mrs. Pearson, I don't think you'll live to see another Christmas."

"So, what do we do now?"

"I'm going to set you up with an oncologist who will discuss medicines and therapies with you. We'll do our best to make you comfortable and able to function as long as possible." He rose, saying, "You may have this room to talk for as long as you need it."

After he left, Mom stared at the table for a full minute. She firmly set her jaw as she processed what she'd just heard. She shook her head back and forth. "He's wrong, you know. I know for a fact I *will* see another Christmas."

The certainty of her words struck me. "How do you know that, Mom?"

"Because this is the year." Seeing that I didn't understand, she continued. "Jimmy, you once asked me what year your father would come

TWO DREAMS & OTHER TALES
My Father's Promise

home. Well, this is it. He'll be home for Christmas this year and I will be there to meet him."

I wanted to be angry at the resurfacing of this unwanted fantasy, but I couldn't get there. I had just learned my mother was going to die—at a relatively young age. The grief I felt overpowered my impulse toward anger, leaving only despair. It didn't escape me that my mother's statement did not have the carefree quality it always had before. She was serious and resolved. I knew this would be a very long year.

I learned my wife wasn't just an angel; she was an angel of mercy. She would not agree to move Mom into any type of clinical care facility. We would move her into our own home and care for her ourselves. I wouldn't have asked her to sacrifice that much, but I gratefully accepted. The new arrangement was difficult for us, but we made the best of it. I worked each day, so Rachel cared for Mom with regular help from a visiting nurse. At night, we cared for her together; me taking the lead, with Rachel resting as much as she could. Even the kids got into the act. Though their grandmother was sick, they loved keeping her company when she was well enough to have them around. She loved giving them her attention and getting theirs in return.

As for her health, that was a continuously changing story. Her strength waned as the months passed, as did her appetite. She also spent more time in bed, as opposed to sitting in her reclining chair. We noted her days had distinct qualities. She had good days when she was lucid and engaged. She also had bad days when she wanted to sleep or just be alone. Over time, the good days became fewer and fewer.

In July, I sensed that the progress of Mom's illness had changed. The good days began to come more frequently again. She wasn't getting better, but she was no longer getting worse. We'd reached some sort of plateau. Her outlook changed as well. She would talk about events the next week, the next month, and even the next year, like she planned to be present for all of them. More than once, I wondered what was sustaining her, but I suspected I already knew. It seemed best to stay away from that subject.

In October, something unexpected happened. One day, a gentleman from the U.S. State Department called me at my office and told me he had

TWO DREAMS & OTHER TALES
My Father's Promise

news of my father. He had been seeking my mother, but could not locate her. I told him she was gravely ill and living with me. He reported that a group of hikers had found the wreckage of a World War II era B-25 bomber in thick undergrowth on the side of a German mountain. It was my father's plane and the remains of him and his crew were still in it.

It's hard to explain the emotions that arise when an intensely painful mystery comes to a sudden and unexpected end. I had so many questions, but I waited to hear the rest. He told me that repatriating my father and his crew would take time. The mountain in question was in East Germany, behind what was now known as the Iron Curtain. You may recall that the year 1962 came at the height of the Cold War. With the erecting of the Berlin Wall the previous August, Germany was one of the active fronts in this ongoing war of words—and bullets—between West and East. Diplomacy and trade still took place, always accompanied by self-serving rhetoric and political posturing. In this case, political concessions would be granted. Money would change hands—as foreign aid. The public show of goodwill by the East would receive an equally public show of appreciation by the West. Everybody would get something. Then, the lost heroes would come home.

The troublesome question for me now was knowing how much to tell my mother. What effect would this have on her and her illness? Was she ready for the truth that Dad was dead? What if she refused to accept that? What if she maintained her determination to see him come home for Christmas? In the end, I decided to wait, and told her nothing.

Less than a week later, the Cold War intervened again. News broke about the discovery of Russian nuclear missiles in Cuba, threatening America's security. Our country and Russia stared one another down—politically and militarily—as the world stood on the brink of war. The State Department man called me again and explained to me about diplomatic priorities. Important as it was, reclaiming six missing World War II airmen was a small matter in the overall scheme of things. My father and his crew would have to wait. However, by November, the crisis was over and the discussions were back on.

TWO DREAMS & OTHER TALES
My Father's Promise

In the first week of December, the word I was waiting for came. Eighteen years after his death, my father was coming home. After all the protocols were observed, he would be sent back to us, arriving by plane on December 20.

"My goodness," I thought aloud, "Dad really *is* coming home for Christmas. What will Mom say about that?"

It was important to me to tell her myself before the television or somebody calling on the telephone did. I rushed home at midday to find her having one of her good days, reading a magazine while sitting in her chair. She looked up and smiled. "Hello, darling," she said, "Aren't you home early?"

"Yes, Mom, I am," I said, trying not to let my anxiety show. "I have news. Very good news." She said nothing and just waited for the rest. For a few seconds, the words wouldn't come. Finally, I said, "I got word from the government today. Dad's coming home for Christmas."

She smiled even more brightly. "Of course, he is," she replied. "He said he would."

Then came the hard part. I took a shaky breath, trying to steel myself. "Mom, you understand he's dead, don't you?"

She gave me a surprised look, then grinned. "Of course, I understand, dear, though it took me a long time to admit it to myself."

What followed was a very awkward conversation. I confessed my long-held and apparently mistaken belief that she was delusional, perhaps even mentally ill. To my surprise, she laughed out loud and told me I wasn't entirely wrong on that point. She could not explain her conviction, but she'd somehow always *known* my father's words were the truth. Common sense and intellect dictated that he was dead, but how could he be and still keep his promise? Her constant reassurances to me were wishful thinking, and perhaps delusional.

My display of anger over the matter brought her out of her dreamlike state and to the point of accepting that she was a widow. It also alerted her to the fact that I wasn't of the same mind as her on this prophecy business—

TWO DREAMS & OTHER TALES
My Father's Promise

or whatever you'd call it. It was embarrassment and pride that drove us apart. Amidst the explanations and apologies, we also realized that we had become estranged because neither of us had ever completed the grieving process—and never experienced it together. That afternoon, we shed a lot of tears as we reminisced about Dad. We talked about our shared pain over losing him and about the good times we had when we were still a family of three.

Two weeks later, Rachel and I bundled Mom up for an hour's drive to the air base for Dad's arrival. I tried to talk her out of going along, but she was adamant. She sat in the wheelchair we brought for her and watched with tremendous emotion as the military transport plane came in and landed. The honor guard brought the flag-draped coffin off the plane and loaded it into a hearse for the drive home. There was plenty of press on hand to record the event. Because of Mom's illness, we opted not to have a military funeral. Instead, a uniformed delegation gave us a short impromptu ceremony there at the airfield. A senior officer produced and read a crisply worded letter from President Kennedy, expressing the nation's gratitude for my father's service and sacrifice. They also presented Mom with my father's Purple Heart and Distinguished Flying Cross.

It turned out my mother hadn't been entirely right, nor had her doctor been entirely wrong. She didn't live to see Christmas that year. Four days after Dad's arrival, I buried both of my parents in a family plot next to the church they were married in and attended. It was Christmas Eve 1962, my twenty-eighth birthday. My mother was fifty-two years old when she died; my father just thirty-four.

For years afterward, I pondered several tough questions. Were those words my father uttered that March morning in 1942 some sort of prophecy or just a whimsical statement intended to make my mother feel better? Was my father's return at Christmas two decades later a fulfillment of prophecy or just a coincidence? Was my mother so connected to my late father that she knew without question the truth of his words? Is such a thing even possible? While I do not subscribe to the beliefs of psychics and spiritualists, my religious beliefs do not automatically tempt me to use words like 'prophecy' and 'miracle' when discussing such events. After

TWO DREAMS & OTHER TALES
My Father's Promise

long consideration, I've come to a place where I am content to let the amazing story of my father's life and death—and his promise—remain a mystery.

TWO DREAMS & OTHER TALES
My Father's Promise

Acknowledgements

I wish to acknowledge those who have read all or part of the manuscript for this collection and provided helpful suggestions, including: Cheryl, Ellen, Barbara, John, and Dave.

About the Author

Greg Treakle was born and raised in southern New Hampshire but has lived and worked in the Northern Neck of Virginia for more than forty years. He received a degree in Mathematics from Virginia Tech in 1984 and spent his career working for the US Department of the Navy. After retiring from government service, he self-published his first novel in 2022. *Two Dreams & Other Tales* is his second publication.

TWO DREAMS & OTHER TALES

Made in the USA
Middletown, DE
11 April 2024

52914357R00089